It was only mid-morning, the Thursday before Memorial Day, and the day was already promising to be hot. I wanted to be floating along the Sometimes Raging Rapids that circled the outer perimeter of the park. For the adventuresome, it offered a detour through rushing waters and over short, plunging falls. When I was in the water, I was adventuresome.

Out of it . . . not so much.

Read all the
MAKING A SPLASH
books!

MAKING A SPLASH #1
Robyn

MAKING A SPLASH #2
Caitlin

MAKING A SPLASH #3
Whitney

Also by Jade Parker

TO CATCH A PIRATE

MAKING A SPLASH
Robyn

MAKING A SPLASH
Robyn

JADE PARKER

Point

For Abby and Morgan,
who went above and beyond.
With deepest appreciation.

Copyright © 2008 by Jan Nowasky

All rights reserved. Published by Point, an imprint of Scholastic Inc., *Publishers since 1920.* SCHOLASTIC, POINT, and associated logos are trademarks and/or registered trademarks of Scholastic Inc.

No part of this publication may be reproduced, stored in a retrieval system, or transmitted in any form or by any means, electronic, mechanical, photocopying, recording, or otherwise, without written permission of the publisher. For information regarding permission, write to Scholastic Inc., Attention: Permissions Department, 557 Broadway, New York, NY 10012.

ISBN-13: 978-0-545-04540-7
ISBN-10: 0-545-04540-1

12 11 10 9 8 7 6 5 4 3 2 1   8 9 10 11 12 13/0

Printed in the U.S.A.
First printing, May 2008

Book design by Steve Scott

CHAPTER ONE

"*Brawk!* Welcome to Paradise Falls! *Brawk!*"

With my large tote bag slung over my shoulder, I looked up at the parrot sitting on a swing hanging from a tall pole. A leather leash kept him tethered to the swing. My best friend Caitlin Morgan, her brother Sean, and I had just passed through the entrance to Paradise Falls water park.

A sign warned not to feed the parrot. Still, Sean reached up and offered the bird some sort of treat.

"*Brawk!* Thanks, mate. *Brawk!*"

Sean grinned. "I taught him that last summer when I worked here and taking care of him was part of my duties."

"Isn't that against park rules, to feed him?" Caitlin asked.

"The rules apply to guests, not employees," Sean said.

Sean had this real *Men in Black* thing going. Black jeans. Black T-shirt that was maybe a size too small and showed off the muscles that I knew he'd been working out to get. He had black hair that fell across his brow. All that black made his startling blue eyes really stand out — when his eyes were visible. Right now they were hidden behind dark sunglasses. But then so were mine and Caitlin's. We'd been to the water park enough times as guests to know that the sun reflecting off the water and cement was glaringly bright.

"It's so quiet," Caitlin said as we followed the path to the main part of the park. "It's kinda eerie."

We heard no screams as people hurtled

down the slides. No splashes as people hit the water. No yells. Nothing. But then the water park wouldn't officially open for the summer for another hour.

"Enjoy it," Sean said. "It's my favorite time, right before the madness starts."

We rounded a corner and the smell of chlorine hit me. I loved it. It called to the water sprite in me. There was nothing I enjoyed more than playing in water.

"Okay, I've got to go to the manager's office," Sean said. "Y'all wait here."

"We know," Caitlin said. "We read our letters."

She really didn't like him telling her what to do. He was two years older than us and had worked here the past two summers. He'd just been promoted to supervisor. I wasn't sure how that was going to work out, because now he had a reason to tell her what to do — and she had to do it.

This summer, Caitlin and I were also working here. Our letters of employment had told us when to arrive and where to wait. Plus a banner that read SUMMER EMPLOYEES WAIT HERE was hanging between two palm trees.

"Just don't get into any trouble," Sean said.

"Like we would," Caitlin mumbled.

"Yeah, you would," he muttered before walking off.

Watching as he disappeared into a building, I wondered why he never talked to me. This morning, when they'd come to pick me up, I'd slid into the backseat with a brightly delivered "Hey!" I was pumped about our first day at work. Caitlin had turned around in the seat and given me a knuckle rap.

Sean had simply grunted. Maybe he wasn't a morning person, or maybe he didn't like me. Whenever I was visiting at Caitlin's if I walked into a room and he was there, he'd mumble something and walk out. On the other hand, he was giving me a ride to work, so who knew? He'd never been mean to me or anything. We just had this strange ignore-each-other relationship going on.

"You know I had to make his lunch this morning," Caitlin said like she was totally disgusted. "It's the price I have to pay for him to drive us here every day."

"That doesn't seem fair. I mean, he works here, too. He has to come here anyway."

"What can I say? My brother's a total jerk." She looked around. "So what do we do now?"

Caitlin had been my best friend since kindergarten. We did everything together, including taking a Red Cross class and getting CPR-certified so we'd be qualified to work here. We wanted to be lifeguards, but a lot of other positions were available at the water park: ride attendants, cleanup, food service, customer service, shop clerks. It was amazing, really.

"We wait, I guess. I wonder where everyone else is," I said.

"They'll be here. We're just early because

Sean had to go to a" — she made quote marks with her fingers — "supervisors' meeting. He's already throwing it in my face that he's going to be in charge of me."

As soon as she'd heard that she was hired, she'd cut her black hair so it was cropped all over, uneven lengths that really worked for her. If it got wet, all she had to do was fluff it with her fingers to make it look good. I'd considered cutting my long brown hair, but I liked having long hair. It was layered but I could still pull it back into a ponytail — which is what I'd done this morning.

"You mean, like, he'll be your supervisor?" I asked.

"I don't think he can be mine. I think there are rules against that. You know how he is, though. He thinks he's important now."

"Well, he is. He's a supervisor." I was impressed anyway.

"Are you defending him? What are you? His lawyer?"

"What? No. I'm just saying. He's young to be a supervisor. Aren't most in college?"

"I guess. Just don't say anything that'll make it go to his head. He's hard enough to live with."

I was ready to drop the subject, so I looked around, even though I knew almost every aspect of the park. Caitlin and I had spent a lot of time here.

Behind me, the locker rooms were camouflaged to look like grass huts. To my right were several souvenir shops and a food court — also sporting a tropical-island atmosphere. Palm trees dotted the path, interspersed with shade trees. As a rule we didn't have palm trees in north Texas, but they looked like they belonged — probably because the entire park had the tropics theme going.

Caitlin sighed. "Think anyone would notice if we sneaked over to Tsunami and just stuck our toes in the water?"

The pool that created awesome eight-foot

waves was ahead of us. The sun glistened off the calm water.

"It's a little hard to get there without leaving footprints in the sand."

In front of Tsunami was the lounging deck, with real sand spread around the lounge chairs. I'm not talking sprinkled sand. I'm talking a foot of sand, enough so you could build sand castles and dig for buried treasure. Sometimes they hid cheap gold trinkets in the sand. You never knew when or where, but you'd hear someone yell when he found one.

"It might be harder to work here than I thought," Caitlin said. "It's so tempting to play."

"No kidding."

Behind the deck was the large, covered pavilion. On the other side of the deck, I could see the upwardly curving path that marked the beginning of Thrill Hill where the larger, more exciting slides waited.

We heard the parrot squawk, no doubt signaling the arrival of someone else.

"I think it would drive me crazy to work near the entrance," Caitlin said. "I might end up strangling that bird."

I smiled. I'm not usually a violent person, but I think the bird could challenge my patience.

A couple of guys emerged from the shadowy walkway. They grinned, looked a little self-conscious, and walked over to the side.

"Summer employees, you think?" Caitlin asked.

"Probably."

They were wearing shorts, T-shirts, and sandals. Caitlin and I were wearing shorts and spaghetti-strap tops. We'd been a little nervous about our first day at work, so we'd talked last night and decided we'd wear something similar — that way if we were dressed wrong, at least we wouldn't be alone in looking silly.

She'd asked Sean what to wear, but he'd only said, "You're working at a water park. What do you think you wear?"

Sean wasn't really into fashion. As a matter of a fact, I'd never seen him wear anything that wasn't black.

It was only mid-morning, the Thursday before Memorial Day, and the day was already promising to be hot. I wanted to be floating along the Sometimes Raging Rapids that circled the outer perimeter of the park. For the adventuresome, it offered a detour through rushing waters and over short, plunging falls. When I was in the water, I was adventuresome. Out of it . . . not so much.

Although my favorite ride was Screaming Falls. For that wicked ride, you stepped into a box and the attendant pushed a button. The floor dropped out and you plummeted down an almost vertical slide, screaming all the way. It was awesome.

See? Adventuresome.

The parrot began seriously squawking, over and over, as more people began to arrive. I recognized a couple of kids from school, but most of the people gathering in the area were strangers.

A low hum vibrated around us as people talked quietly. People were clustering in small groups, probably friends, just like Caitlin and me. We were our own little clique. Sometimes I thought we needed to grow a bit, but Caitlin didn't see the point. "We'd have to start taking votes on things," she'd said. "You know, be democratic. I'd rather be queen."

She always said it jokingly, but it was true. Usually Caitlin came up with the ideas, and I simply followed. The arrangement worked for us, because Caitlin liked to lead, and, well, I didn't.

I was actually a little nervous about how I might respond in a crisis. I was pretty sure I could handle it, but I'd never been tested. I was really hoping that Caitlin and I would be working in the same area, would be paired up, partners.

Glancing around, I saw a girl sitting on a bench by herself. I hadn't seen her come in. She had long, flowing blond hair. Park employee rules were that long hair had to be pulled back — I guess if it was whipping around your face you might have a problem seeing everything you needed to see.

Anyway, the girl was wearing large sunglasses that made her look like an actress or a supermodel. Or maybe it was the fact that she appeared to be totally bored. I wondered if she was here for a photo shoot. She just didn't look like the type to work at a water park. Didn't look like the type to work at all, actually. I'm not sure what it was about her that gave me that impression. She seemed aloof, not at all customer-oriented. Plus, she had a large leather tote bag resting near her feet. Who brought leather to a water park?

I noticed a lone guy with short-cropped dark hair standing nearby, watching her like maybe he wanted to go talk to her, but was too shy. Whenever she glanced over at him, he looked away. It was kinda funny in a sad sort of way. Reminded me of me, I guess.

I tended to look away from guys when they looked at me, like maybe they'd know what I'd been thinking as I watched them. I was fifteen and wasn't all that comfortable talking to guys. Caitlin was better at it, because she at least had a brother to practice on. I was an only child.

Mom had fallen in love with my dad in high school. They got married right after they graduated. After I was born, Dad decided there was more to life than family and working at the neighborhood convenience store. So he and Mom had gotten divorced.

And he'd headed off into the sunset.

Total loser. I hated to admit that since half of me was carrying his genes. But he was. Mom and I had never heard from him again. Not even child support payments.

When I was younger, I pretended he was in the Witness Protection Program. That he never contacted us because he wanted to protect us from the bad guys he was running from. But eventually I had to face reality:

We weren't in danger, Dad wasn't trying to protect us. He was just ignoring us.

Mom was still a little guy-shy. And who could blame her? Maybe I'd taken after her, was a little guy-shy, too.

"You know we could meet a lot of guys this summer," Caitlin whispered. "Wouldn't it be awesome if we got a boyfriend?"

"You mean one to share?" I asked, teasing her.

"No, one each." She didn't smile or laugh at my joke. She was getting pretty tired of being boyfriend-less. "I read an article about summer romances. You have to be so careful because sometimes guys don't take them seriously."

She was also always looking for the answers to life in teen magazines.

"Isn't that like when you meet someone on vacation?" I asked.

"Well, yeah."

"All these people live around here."

"So you think we're safe from getting hurt?"

"Maybe. I don't know. It's just that he won't be going away."

"Unless he's a college guy," she said.

"Yeah, right, Mom's going to let me date a college guy."

Behind us, I heard a door slam shut. An older man wearing red shorts and a white polo shirt with the words PARADISE FALLS and a little waterfall embroidered on it strode through the crowd. He smiled, said hi, patted a shoulder here and there. A line of boys and girls, that included Sean, followed him.

The man hopped onto a bench in front of us the way some kids jumped onto their skateboards. So maybe he wasn't as old as I thought he was.

"Welcome to Paradise Falls!"

The kids who had been following him lined up on either side of the bench. I figured they were all the supervisors.

"I like to introduce myself as Mr. T," the guy on the bench said. "It's simpler than my real name, which you either won't remember or will butcher trying to pronounce." He laughed, and I wondered if he was one of those people who laugh at their own jokes, mostly because no one else does.

"I'm the park's general manager," he continued. "We have our permanent employees who are in charge of various aspects of the park. You may or may not meet them. Then we have our summer supervisors, who you will come to know.

"Our job here — *your* job here — is to make sure our guests feel like they've stepped into paradise. Keeping them happy is our number one priority, that and keeping them safe. That's a big responsibility, but we know you're up to it or we wouldn't have hired you.

"My assistant, Gretchen, has your assignments" — a young woman with blond hair standing beside him waved her hand — "and once she passes those out, you'll report to the customer service hut where we'll pass out your uniforms. Enjoy the summer." He pointed a finger at us, to dramatically emphasize his next words. "But mostly, be *watchful* out there."

He hopped off the bench, and Gretchen climbed up. She smiled brightly. "All righty! Here we go!" She began calling out names and handing out the envelopes.

It was several minutes before she called out, "Caitlin Morgan!"

Caitlin released a little squeal like she'd just been announced the winner at the MTV Awards. She hurried forward to get her envelope.

"What did you get?" I asked her as soon as she came back to me.

"I thought I'd wait until you get yours."

"Don't you want to know, like now?"

"Well, yeah, but —"

"Robyn Johnson!"

My heart slammed against my ribs. This was it. I edged my way past the people who were too interested in reading about their own assignments to really notice me. I wiped my hands on my shorts before taking the envelope.

I thought Sean was looking at me. It was a little hard to tell with his sunglasses. I smiled. He didn't smile back. Okay, so he wasn't looking at me. Or maybe he took his job too seriously to smile. Either way, I felt a little silly as I went back to where Caitlin waited.

She grabbed my arm and pulled me off to the side, away from everyone else.

"Who should go first?" she asked, studying the envelope in her hand.

"You," I told her.

"Okay." She tore off the end of the envelope, blew into it — no doubt to build the suspense — then tipped it so the slip of paper fell into her hand. She turned slightly so I could read it at the same time that she did. She was just a little shorter than me, which made reading over her shoulder easy. She unfolded the paper —

"Yes!" she said before I got a chance to see what it said. "Tsunami! Hottie heaven! Yes, yes, yes!"

"That totally rocks!" I said. Wow. What could be better than being paid to hang out where the cute guys were?

She was grinning broadly when she turned to me. "Let's see what you've got," she said.

I couldn't believe how nervous I was. My first job ever! I'd remember this summer forever.

I slid my fingernail beneath the flap, worked it free, and pulled out the sheet of paper. I unfolded it and stared at the bolded words. "Splash? What is Splash?"

I didn't remember ever slipping and sliding my way along that slide. Was it new? Obviously, it created a splash, so it was probably a big ride, maybe a large waterfall or a multistory vertical drop —

"Oh, no! Isn't that in the kiddie area?" Caitlin asked.

My stomach dropped down to my toes like the floor at Screaming Falls had just opened beneath me. "Kiddie area? Do they even need lifeguards in Mini Falls? Aren't the parents still watching the kids?"

"They have lifeguards everywhere. Liability issues." She moved to the large board where a huge map of the park indicated where we were. It had the typical "You are here," with a red arrow. Caitlin studied it for a minute, then pressed her finger to the area on the other side of the park designated as Mini Falls. "There. It is."

"Well, somebody's got to work it," I said, determined to put a positive spin on this. Whenever Mom and I drove anywhere, she'd listen to CDs about the power of positive thinking. I wanted to stay positive. But most of the guys who hung out in that area would be, like, forty-two inches *short* or shorter. And still hanging out with their mommies.

"But you'll be working with *him*!" Caitlin exclaimed.

"Him? Him who?"

"Sean. He'll be your supervisor. That's his area. I know, because I overheard him complaining about it to someone. I mean, no one wants to work there. It's miserable. Whining babies and all that."

"You know, you're really depressing me here."

"I'm sorry. It's just so awful. It's easier to work for people you don't know, people who have no expectations about you."

"Sean has expectations about me?"

"Probably. Don't you think? He knows everything about you."

"Everything?"

"He's known you as long as I have."

"Still, there are things he doesn't know." Lots of things.

I wanted a loophole. A way out of this disaster. I really thought I could have handled being around kids all day — but being around Sean Morgan? *I don't think so!*

I mean, I knew him. He knew me. It would be weird — especially since, like I mentioned, we had this whole avoidance thing going.

"But isn't there some sort of rule about

people who know each other not working together?"

"Family members can't work in the same area. You're not family."

"Yes, I am. Sorta. We're sisters of the heart."

"I don't think that counts."

I looked at the paper again. My assignment hadn't changed. How bad could it be?

"So, we'll hook up at lunch at the lounging deck in the Tsunami area, because sorry — no way am I going to Mini Falls where all the babies are. Okay?" Caitlin asked.

"Sure."

I picked up my tote bag and slung it over my shoulder. "Guess we need to go get our uniforms."

I was nothing if I wasn't an optimist. I was certain I'd discover some advantage to working in this particular area. Still, I was having a difficult time imagining what it could be.

CHAPTER TWO

Splash. Basically, it was a little twelve-inch-deep wading pool at the bottom of a winding slide. At the top, water swirled through a very shallow pool and over the slide. Nearby was a large mesh container that contained inner tubes. We grabbed a tube and put it at the top of the four-foot-high slide. A kid wearing a life preserver climbed onto it. Then we gently pushed him off the landing and he glided toward the water.

Splash!

Another lifeguard — and sometimes a parent if the kiddos were really small — stood near the bottom of the slide but within easy reach just in case a child toppled. But that rarely happened. It was the shortest slide in the park, specially designed to give the little tykes a safe thrill.

It wasn't very challenging work, but then my concern wasn't the work so much as the supervisor. I really didn't want Sean judging me. Caitlin was right. It would be weird.

I'd gone to the locker room, found my locker, and changed into my uniform — a red tank bathing suit and red visor. I had a whistle draped around my neck. My red hippack was buckled securely. Attached to it was my park photo ID. Lying off to the side, a little away from the water, but within easy reach, was my red rescue tube. I was prepared. Totally.

But still, the excitement factor here was going to be negative twenty and falling faster than someone shooting down the Bermuda Triangle — which was almost a total vertical drop until the slide suddenly wasn't anymore and you were, like, hurtling through the air, before you disappeared into the twelve-foot pool beneath you.

Big difference between twelve inches and twelve feet — not to mention the guys who hang out at each one. As much as I hated to admit it, because it made me seem so shallow — pun intended — I was disappointed in the guy factor here. I'd thought it would be fun to work someplace where I was paid to keep an eye on cute guys.

"Hey."

I looked over. A blond guy in red swim trunks and a visor that matched mine walked over and placed his hands on his hips. He was cute in a chipmunk kind of way. He had really puffy cheeks when he smiled, and he was smiling now.

"Hi," I said.

"I'm Nick."

"Robyn." The conversationally challenged, apparently.

He looked around. "So who did we tick off to get this gig, huh?"

I laughed, not sure what to say to that. I mean, yeah, it was a lousy job but complaining wasn't going to change anything.

"Have you worked here before — at the park, I mean?" he asked.

I shook my head. "First time."

"Me, too. So maybe it's just a matter of working our way up to the cool rides."

"Maybe." But if that was the case, then Caitlin would be suffering beside me. Although, technically, she wasn't at a ride.

"I spent a lot of time here last summer," Nick said. "It all looks different, though."

"You spent time in the kiddie area?"

He laughed. He had a great laugh, and I thought working with him could be fun. He seemed easy to talk to.

"No way. Never even got close. Nah, I don't know what it is. Maybe it's just because there's no one here yet."

Well, except for the employees, of course. But I guess we didn't count.

I caught sight of Sean swaggering in our direction. He was in his red Paradise Falls swim trunks, with a whistle draped around his neck, tapping against his bare chest. His attention was focused on the girl walking beside him. They were talking, he was smiling. He never smiled at me like that.

As they got closer, I recognized her. She was the blond I'd noticed earlier, the one who'd been sitting by herself, looking bored. She was decked out in the official Paradise Falls uniform and had her hair pulled back now. So I guess she wasn't a supermodel. She was just like the rest of us.

Sean pointed toward me, said something that made her smile and made me suddenly feel self-conscious. What was there to say about me?

He led her over. She was smaller than I was. Slender. Petite. Her large, really dark-lensed sunglasses made it look like she was trying to hide.

"Hey, Robyn, Nick, this is Whitney. She's going to work at Splash."

Apparently, she needed a personal escort.

"Hey," Nick said, his smile even bigger than it had been when he was talking to me.

"Park will be opening in fifteen. Got any questions?" Sean asked.

Nick and I shook our heads. Whitney just sighed.

"Okay then. To start with, a couple of you help the kids climb into a tube at the top, one catches 'em if they spill over at the bottom. Think you can handle it?"

Was that a serious question?

I nodded. "Yeah, of course."

"Okay then."

"Okay then" seemed to be all he could think to say to signal that we were good to go. I wondered if he was as nervous about being my supervisor as I was about having him as my supervisor.

"So, Nick, why don't you start out at the bottom of the slide?" Sean suggested. "Every fifteen minutes we'll rotate positions so no one falls asleep. Then we've got what we call rotators who'll come through and relieve you for break and lunch."

"Awesome," Nick said, before hopping on the slide and riding down to the bottom, fake-screaming like he was terrified.

I laughed. Sean cleared his throat. I stopped laughing. This was serious business. For a minute, I'd gotten caught up in the fun and forgotten.

"Hey, Nick, we're not supposed to actually play on the slides," Sean called out.

"I wasn't playing, dude," Nick said. "I was transporting."

"Yeah, right," Sean grumbled. He looked at me and Whitney. "Okay then, if you've got no questions, I've got other areas to watch, employees to supervise, so I'll check back later."

He waited a second to see if we had questions. We didn't. Then he walked away.

As soon as he was out of sight, Whitney sat down on the edge of the pool, near the slide. She waved at Nick. He waved back. Then she put her arms behind her, leaned back, and began kicking her feet in the water, creating little splashes.

It seemed like if we were going to work together that we should at least be friendly — like lab partners at school. It was easier to work with someone you knew. Not easier if he was your supervisor, but easier if you were equals. And Whitney and I were equals, working in the same position. Who knew? Maybe we could even be friends.

"So have you worked here before?" I asked Whitney.

She scoffed. "No."

"So where were you hoping to work?"

"Why would anyone *hope* to work anywhere?"

"I mean, if you could work anywhere in the park you wanted, where would you want to be assigned?"

"Ooh, toughie. Let me see. How 'bout *nowhere*?"

What was her problem?

"Look, I don't mean to be nosy, but with your attitude, it's like you don't want to work."

"Right on."

"Then why are you here?" I asked.

"My dad's making me." She looked around and pointed. "Any idea who that is?"

I glanced over to where she was pointing. It was the guy from this morning, the one I'd seen watching her. He was working the ice-cream cart, wearing red shorts and a white polo shirt with the little Paradise Falls logo on it.

"No," I said. "I saw him this morning, though."

"Yeah, I did, too. He kept looking at me."

"Maybe he thinks you're cute."

"Well, yeah, of course. Who doesn't?"

Maybe me?

Reaching up, she released her hair and shook her head, sending the long strands flying before settling back again. "I guess as far as jobs go, this one isn't too bad. I can improve my tan, play in the water, watch cute guys walk by."

She already had an end-of-summer tan. I didn't know how she thought she'd improve it. As for cute guys walking by, most were at the age where they still waddled.

And speaking of waddlers . . . I spotted a group of about a dozen kids walking toward Splash. They were trudging along in a single line, all holding on to a length of jump rope — a lady at each end. I'd seen groups like them plenty last year. They were day-care kids, on a field trip.

I looked at Whitney. "Looks like we're about to get busy."

She pushed her sunglasses down her nose. She had the greenest eyes I'd ever seen. "You don't really expect me to help, do you?"

"Uh, well, yeah."

She shook her head. "Think again."

"You're gonna get fired," I felt a need to point out.

"No, I won't." She nudged her sunglasses back into place. "I'm just so adorable. I can do anything I want and never get in trouble."

Great. Just the type of person I wanted to be around all summer.

I heard several screeches and turned back to the day-care kids who were scrambling up the steps to the slide.

"No running!" I yelled down.

But they kept coming at the speed of light.

Wasn't this summer going to be all about fun?

CHAPTER THREE

"Whitney really thinks she doesn't have to do anything," I told Caitlin when I met her for lunch.

We were sitting on lounge chairs on the sandy deck at Tsunami.

"Tell Sean," Caitlin said, slathering sunblock on her legs.

"I don't want him to think I'm a whiner."

"What do you care what he thinks about you?"

I couldn't explain it. I'd sorta always cared what he thought. Maybe because he was older and I thought if he liked me, then maybe other guys would like me. I guess maybe I saw him as my litmus test. I don't know. I probably knew him better than I knew any other guy — but still, I knew him hardly at all.

I put my beach bag — a red one that I'd recently bought to match my red uniform — in my lap and started digging around for my soda. I popped the top, took a long swallow, and set it aside. I pulled out the small, insulated bag where I'd packed my peanut butter and jelly sandwich, along with a small tub of fruit. I hadn't figured out yet how to make an interesting lunch. All my years in school, I'd been on the cafeteria plan. Mom thought it ensured I ate healthy. *Ha!*

"Seriously," Caitlin said. "He's being paid to be the bad guy. Let him yell at her. It's not fair to you if she's not pulling her weight."

"I guess." Not that there was a lot of weight to pull at Splash. Quite honestly, I could handle it by myself. But still . . .

I glanced around and spotted Sean sitting at a table beneath an umbrella. "Although I'm really not sure my talking to him is going to do any good."

"Why not?" Caitlin asked.

"Because he's eating lunch with her."

Caitlin glanced over her shoulder. "That's Whitney? That blond?"

"Yeah."

"How many bleach strips does she use? I mean, really, have you ever seen teeth that white?"

"You should see them when the sun bounces off them — or her gold watch. It's blinding. I think the watch is a Cartier."

"No way."

"Looks like it."

"Why would she wear it to a water park?"

"I don't know, Caitlin. I can't figure her out."

She studied them for a minute. "Looks like he's actually talking to her. He's smiling.

I wonder if she's the girl he's been dreaming about."

"He talks to you about girls?"

"No, but he doesn't always close his door when he's on the phone, and if I need to stop in the hallway and catch my breath on my way to my bedroom" — she shrugged — "you know, sometimes I can't help but hear things."

I laughed. She could be so outrageous. So without remorse. She was always spying on him, and then telling me what she'd found out.

"Anyway, I heard him telling someone that a new cute babe was going to start working at the park this year. Sounded like maybe he was really interested. Maybe it's her," Caitlin said.

Whitney laughed at something Sean said.

"She seems to like him," I muttered, wondering why it bothered me.

"He can be pretty entertaining when he wants to be." She twisted back around and lay back. "So you're probably right. Complaining to him might not get you anywhere, but still you need to tell him. It's his job."

"It's not like it's hard work or anything. It's just the principle of the thing. You know?"

"I hear you, girlfriend."

What was it about Whitney that he liked? Other than the fact that, as she so succinctly put it, she was adorable? I wasn't hideous or anything, but I didn't think I'd ever announce — especially to someone I'd just met — that I was cute.

"Okay, check out that guy," Caitlin said, bringing my attention back to the reason we were eating lunch at Tsunami. Because of the scenery. Working at a water park gave us the real lowdown on how fit guys were.

The guy in question was obviously a lifeguard, walking along the edge of the pool. He had brown hair. He looked like he was a little older than us. Totally cute.

"So what do you think?" Caitlin asked.

"Huh?"

"His kiss factor. What would you rate him, on a scale of one to ten? One being a toad. Ten being Zac Efron."

"But a frog can turn into a prince."

Yes, I was a hopeless romantic.

"You know what I mean. Would you kiss him?"

I considered her question, considered the guy. I nodded. "Yeah, probably." Maybe. I don't know. The real question was: Would he kiss me?

"Yeah, me too."

"Are you interested in him?" I asked.

"I don't know. Maybe. Wish we had a way to meet all the guys at once so we could narrow down our choices."

"Do you really think it's a good idea to date someone we work with?"

"Sure. Why not?"

"Well, if things don't work out, we'll see him every day."

She shrugged. "We just have to make sure things work out."

She sounded so confident. It was one of the things I'd always like about Caitlin — she wasn't afraid of anything. She thought she could always succeed. Even if she hadn't had a boyfriend yet. It was just a matter of time.

Caitlin pulled a teen mag out of her tote, opened it to a page she'd marked with a sticky note. "Here's a guide to knowing when you're ready to kiss a guy. There's even a test, so you can score your readiness. I'll read the questions, you give me your answers."

Caitlin was always taking the tests in magazines. If she did as well on her tests at school as she did on the magazine tests, she'd graduate valedictorian.

"Number one. Whenever you see him, *A* your heart pounds, *B* you feel nauseous, *C* you walk in the opposite direction."

I, on the other hand, did horrible on these things. And okay, I usually cheated, looking to see which score I needed to give me the rating that I wanted. "Isn't there an 'all of the above'?" I asked.

"No, you have to choose."

I didn't want to choose. I didn't want to do a stupid test. My supervisor was having lunch with the laziest employee at the park. What were the odds that he might be telling her to get her act in gear?

Or was he agreeing with her — that she was too adorable to believe? And why did I care if he thought she was adorable?

"How 'bout if I give you the test?" I suggested.

"Oh, I already took it," Caitlin said.

"How'd you score?"

"Perfect ten. 'Pucker up, you're ready!'"

I settled back against the lounge chair. "I don't need to take a test. I know the answer. I'm ready, too."

But the thing was, just because I was ready, didn't mean it was going to happen. Because the truth was: It took two.

CHAPTER FOUR

Much to my surprise, that afternoon, time flew. Maybe because I was concentrating on ignoring Whitney as she worked on her tan. Obviously Sean hadn't given her a reality check. So I was the one trying to convince a mother that rushing her bawling son down a slide would not stop him from crying — shouldn't parenting require a license?

The kid was obviously terrified. It was cruel to push him down the slide. I wasn't going to do it. I wasn't going to help her hold him in the tube so he'd learn it wasn't scary. When the mom finally took her upset child away, I turned to find a tall girl with red hair telling me it was time for a break.

Some kid-sized tables with benches were set around the outskirts of our area. I headed for one and sat down. My knees nearly hit my chest. The table had an umbrella canopy so I got some relief from the sun. I removed my tube of sunblock from my hip-pack and started applying it. By the end of summer I was going to be beyond a golden tan.

When I was finished, I put my sunblock away and sat back, absorbing the energy of the park. The cacophony of noises — screams, yells, laughs, splashes — might give some people a headache, but I loved them. They generated excitement, confirmed that people were having a good time, enjoying themselves. From here, I could look in the distance and see some of the huge slides and tubes that gave Thrill Hill its name.

I got one day off a week. I wondered if when that day came around I'd be sick of this place or if I'd want to come here to play.

Right now, I really had an urge to sit in some water and cool off.

I was thinking about taking a walk, wading through Lost Lagoon. It was a large shallow pool in the middle of Mini Falls. A wrecked pirate ship was in the middle. Kids climbed over it. Explored it. Slides brought them back into the water. Water guns were mounted along the deck so kids could spray water on those in the pool.

Sean suddenly appeared and sat at my table on the bench across from me. He slid a little plastic cup of strawberry ice cream toward me. "Here."

"Did you get this from the ice-cream guy?"

"Yeah, Jake. It's no big deal. Employees can have free ice cream or drinks when they're on break. Figured you deserved a treat."

"How did you figure that?"

"Saw you dealing with that mom. What was her problem anyway?"

"She thought her kid was being a *baby*. *Hello?!?* He is a baby."

"They'll let anyone be parents."

His comment gave me a chill since I'd been thinking almost the same thing. I picked up the cup of ice cream. "How did you know strawberry was my favorite?"

"*Puh-leze*. Mom keeps a carton in the freezer with your name on it for when you come over."

I don't know why I was surprised he knew my favorite ice cream. I knew his. I could have told him without looking that he had chocolate.

He took a bite and worked his mouth before asking, "So other than dealing with insane parents, how do you like working here?"

"It's torture. Absolute torture."

He took off his sunglasses. I was always surprised by how blue his eyes were. Caitlin's were, too, but somehow his were a deeper hue. "What's going on? Is someone not working?"

Was he serious? Was he not looking around? Not observing everything? What kind of supervisor was he?

Now was the time to mention Whitney, but in a moment of irony, she was, at that second, helping a kid into a tube. So how could I complain about someone not doing something when she was doing it?

Besides, Sean looked so serious, so concerned, that I felt a little bad for making him worry. And I really didn't want to ruin the moment. It was kinda nice. I'd never had a guy bring me ice cream before.

"No, it's just hard to work with all this water calling to me. Don't you want to be out there making a splash, creating waves, plummeting down slides?"

"You know, since I started working here, I've kinda forgotten how to enjoy it." He shook his head and smiled slightly, like he was amused by the thought. He slipped on his sunglasses and looked out toward the park where all the action was.

Three little kids scampered by. Sean blew his whistle. "No running!"

They stopped immediately, walked for several steps, then ran again.

"Kids," he muttered.

"Caitlin said you didn't want to work in Mini Falls."

"She tells you everything, doesn't she?"

"Pretty much. So where did you want to work?"

"Marketing."

I shook my head. I knew what marketing was, but I didn't know how it worked here. "Where's that?"

"In the main office. You brainstorm ideas, create flyers, help with advertising. You get to be creative. Working the park, there just aren't a lot of ways to tell kids to slow down. It gets a little boring."

Sean was very artistic. He'd taken art classes. His mom had framed some of his work and hung it in their game room, so I knew how talented he was. Plus I'd seen some of his work displayed at school.

"You'd be good with that," I said.

He grinned, a crooked grin, like maybe he was a little embarrassed that I would praise him.

"You think so?" he asked.

"I know so. I've seen your work. You're good."

"Thanks."

We settled into silence. For a few minutes, we simply ate our ice cream. More kids rushed toward where we were sitting, slowed down when they saw us, sped up once they were past — like maybe the rules were "no running if a lifeguard was around, otherwise it was okay." A few older kids were around, obviously babysitting, and a lot of parents, because kids age six and under did have to be accompanied by a parent. Although we did have a Castaway hut where lost — or marooned — kids were taken.

I didn't know how people lost their kids, but they did. On the other hand, if I was the kid whose mom was trying to force me to go down the slide, maybe I'd run away.

"I just want you to know that I can't give you any special treatment," Sean said after a while.

I tapped my spoon against the cup and peered over at him. "Did I ask?"

"No, but, this is awkward."

I didn't get it. "What is?"

He took another bite of ice cream like he needed time to think about his answer.

"My being your supervisor. You being Caitlin's friend. I mean, you're gonna run and tell her everything I do wrong —"

"Wait." I shook my head. "You? Do something wrong?"

"I know. Hard to imagine, but —"

Had I actually teased him and he'd teased back? That was even harder to imagine than him making a mistake.

"*Did* you do something wrong?" I asked.

"No, but I'm the youngest supervisor, so I'm on probation. I can't afford to make any mistakes or to have gossip going around. And I have to give you orders, and I need you to show respect when I do."

"'Show respect'? Who are you? Tony Soprano?"

"There. See? That's exactly what I'm talking about."

I looked down at my bare feet. At his. His were so much bigger. How cool was it to work someplace where no shirts, no shoes were no problem? I lifted my gaze back to his. "Can't you, like, I don't know, get me transferred to another section of the park? One with cooler rides?"

"I already did that for Caitlin. I can't keep asking for favors."

"You got Caitlin that job?"

He suddenly looked embarrassed. He gave a little shrug. "Don't tell her, okay? I mean, it was no big deal. I knew it was the job she wanted, and I didn't want her complaining all summer if she didn't get it. It would make all our lives miserable and you know it."

I felt really disloyal to Caitlin, because I did know it. Still I didn't nod, just sat there waiting for him to continue.

"But I can't keep bugging them about moving people around. Besides, it's your first year. You gotta earn the better jobs."

I almost said, "I have to earn them, but Caitlin doesn't. Not fair." But I didn't. He was just a first-year supervisor. He had limited powers. And quite honestly, I was impressed that he'd gotten Caitlin the job she wanted — even if his reasons weren't the best. He hadn't had to do it.

"So are we cool with this?" he asked.

He didn't want to be my supervisor. I didn't want to work for him. How could we be cool with it? Still, what choice did I have? Unless I went to management and asked for a transfer. They'd want to know why. So I'd either look like someone who didn't work well with others or they'd think he was a bad supervisor, which so far he hadn't been.

"Yeah, okay," I said.

"Good." He scooped up some ice cream. "Thanks. I know it's pretty much one of the worst jobs around. Well, except for picking up trash."

"Nah, it's worse than picking up trash. At least with trash pickup, you get changes of scenery."

And changes in scenery usually included guys a lot older than four.

He grinned. "Yeah, you're right. Loading little snotty-nosed kids — I hated the job."

"You worked it?" I asked, surprised.

"First summer. Thought it would never end."

"Am I going to have to do this the whole summer?"

"Who knows? Maybe I'll have a word with your supervisor."

"You're my supervisor."

He laughed. "Yeah, I know — shoot! I gotta go."

Tossing his ice-cream cup into the trash can as he went past it, he walked over to Lost Lagoon.

A couple of lifeguards — a guy and a girl — were standing there talking, laughing. The guy pulled her close, kissed her.

It was really none of my business, but still I watched as Sean approached them. I'm no expert at reading body language but once Sean broke them up, it was pretty obvious that no one in that little group was happy. The girl finally flounced away. I'd never seen anyone actually flounce before, but it was clear she'd had enough of whatever was being said.

The guy and Sean talked for a little longer. When Sean turned to leave, the guy stuck out his tongue. *Very mature.*

When Sean turned back, the guy looked all innocent.

Until that moment, I hadn't considered how difficult it was to be a supervisor. Sean had probably worked with a lot of these people last summer, and now he had to tell them what to do. And worse than that, he had to get after them if they weren't doing what they were supposed to.

It was strange, because suddenly I wasn't looking at Caitlin's brother anymore.

I was looking at a supervisor. My supervisor.

Tapping the ice-cream cup, I couldn't help but realize that I was actually impressed. How strange was that?

"I couldn't tell Sean about Whitney," I said to Caitlin later when we were in the locker rooms changing out of our uniforms.

"Why not?"

"It just seemed so, I don't know, childish. You know. 'Please, make her work.' I just couldn't do it."

"I'll take care of it," Caitlin said, slipping into her sparkly flip-flops. She was all about the sparklies.

"What? No, don't do that. I'll do it." I slung my tote bag over my shoulder and followed her outside.

"What I don't understand," she said, "is why Sean put you in charge of her."

"I'm not really in charge —"

"I mean, seriously, how many peop[le does] it take to work Splash?"

Okay, she had a point.

"It's like he's picking on you — punishing you for being my friend."

Okay, that seemed a little extreme — the punishing part anyway. But she was right. Until today, Sean had pretty much avoided me. Obviously, I wasn't one of his favorite people, so yeah, maybe he was picking on me a little. But then he'd brought me ice cream, so I really didn't know what to think. Had he done it as a supervisor, Caitlin's brother, or for another reason? To show he liked me?

I was making sharing ice cream way too complicated.

Sean was standing at the gate, talking to Whitney. He said good-bye to her. She gave me a little finger wave that for some reason I didn't quite trust. What had she been telling him? Still I waved back at her, then followed Sean out through the gate.

"So, is *she* your new girlfriend?" Caitlin asked.

"Not that it's any of your business, but no, she's not my girlfriend," Sean said.

"Do you want her to be your girlfriend?" Caitlin asked.

"Okay, see? I try to be nice and answer your questions and then you start getting nosy."

"So, the answer is yes."

Sean glanced over his shoulder at me. "I don't know how you put up with her as a friend."

"Better me as a friend than you as an enemy," Caitlin said.

He snapped his gaze to her. "What does that mean?"

"She told me about you assigning your girlfriend to Splash."

"She's not my girlfriend," Sean repeated.

We'd reached the car, but instead of unlocking the doors he turned to face me. "I thought you'd get along with Whitney."

Suddenly I was the bad guy here?

"We didn't *not* get along. She just sorta has this attitude, like, she doesn't have to do anything."

He shrugged. "Give her a break. She's never worked before."

"Neither have I, but I know I'm not being paid to admire my toes."

His mouth twitched, and I could tell he was trying not to smile.

"Just give her a chance, okay? Seriously, you'll like her once you get to know her."

Which made me wonder if maybe he *did* like her, if maybe he wanted her to be his girlfriend. If maybe she was indeed the cute babe that Caitlin had overheard him talking about.

He didn't wait for my answer, but turned and unlocked the car, which was fine with me, because I wasn't sure what I could say that would make any sense. What made him think Whitney and I had anything in common? Or that we could possibly get along?

CHAPTER FIVE

The next morning I stood in front of my mirror, glaring at my reflection. My job pretty much prevented me from doing anything creative with my hair. The ponytail was so boring.

Maybe I should just lop it off.

And we weren't allowed to add flair to our uniform — unlike some restaurants that required it. So how could I make myself stand out from all the other girls there?

Did I even want to stand out? I was just such a get-lost-in-the-crowd kinda girl. Everyone seemed to notice Whitney — even when she wasn't doing anything. Of course, that seemed to be her normal mode: doing nothing.

Why did it bother me so much that Sean liked her?

I heard the car horn honk.

Ugh! Sean was early.

I hurried down the stairs and grabbed my tote bag from where I'd put it by the door earlier, after making my lunch and stuffing it inside. Mom had already left for work. She was an administrative assistant for one of the CEOs at a computer firm. She never talked much about what she did. Sounded important to me, though. Company initials always did.

I locked the door, rushed down the sidewalk to where the car was idling. I opened the back door and slid inside.

"Hey," I said, a little breathless.

Sean grunted before pulling out onto the street.

Caitlin turned around. "I got a little sunburned yesterday. How about you?"

"Yeah." My skin had felt tight. I was definitely going to apply more lotion today.

It was a totally boring subject, but with Sean in the car, we couldn't talk boys. He'd give us a hard time about it. No question.

We were all pretty quiet on the drive into work. Since it was Friday and we were heading into the weekend, we knew the crowds would be picking up. Tomorrow and Sunday would be out of control — so this was our last chance to catch our breath before it got crazy. We had to arrive a little earlier than most of the employees because Sean had another supervisors' meeting. But I was okay with it, was looking forward to a chance to simply enjoy the silence of the park.

When Caitlin and I walked out of the employee locker rooms after changing into our uniforms, I spotted Sean leaning against the wall — like maybe he'd been waiting for us. He shoved himself away.

"Hey, Robyn, got a sec?"

That made my heart thunder. Why would he want to talk to me? Was it good news — I was being transferred to the Bermuda Triangle? Or bad news — I'd done something wrong? Who fired people? The supervisors or the manager?

"For what?" Caitlin asked.

"None of your business." He jerked his thumb over his shoulder. "Head to work."

"Sean —"

"Come on, Caitlin. I'm talking to you now as a supervisor, not your brother. Get to work."

Caitlin looked at me. "You'll tell me what he says, right?"

Would I? Of course I would. She was my best friend. I nodded. Although it really made me nervous that he was insisting she leave. It couldn't be good.

"There," she said to him, before stomping off.

"She is such a pain," Sean grumbled.

"Maybe it's just that you're so irritating."

Had I really said that? That was kinda

rude, maybe because I was so nervous. But he didn't seem offended. Instead, he said, "Big brothers are supposed to irritate their little sisters. Makes it all even out since they irritate us from the moment they're born."

"I don't really get the whole sibling rivalry thing," I said, trying to delay whatever bad news was coming my way. Maybe if I distracted him, he'd forget what it was he wanted to tell me — alone with no witnesses.

"That's right. I forgot. You don't have any brothers."

"Or sisters," I felt obligated to point out.

"That's right," he said again, like he was a teacher who'd asked a question and I'd gotten it correct. "You're an only child. You don't act like one."

I furrowed my brow. "What does an only child act like?"

"Spoiled, usually."

"Says who?"

"The same people who say older brothers are irritating. Anyway, listen, I have a favor to ask. It's about Whitney. She's feeling, you know, like she doesn't belong, so will you maybe invite her to go with you for lunch?"

"You couldn't ask that with Caitlin around?"

"If she knew I was asking, she'd give me a hard time about it and probably be unfriendly to Whitney — just because it's a favor to me."

I stared at him. "First of all, she wouldn't be unfriendly. She's not a mean person. Second, I don't understand why it's a favor for you, if I invite Whitney to lunch. Do you like her or something?"

"Well, yeah, I like her, and I know she doesn't have the whole work ethic down, but if you could just, you know, be nice to her, include her —"

"You think you have to tell me to be nice?"

"Hey, you hang out with my sister. What else am I supposed to think?"

"You're the one who needs lessons in

'nice.' When I get in the car and say, 'Hey,' as in 'hey, good morning,' 'good day,' 'hello,' you grunt. What's up with that anyway?"

He held up his hands. "Don't go all ballistic on me. I have things on my mind."

"Like what?"

"How to make a good impression as a supervisor. It's not easy, you know. Just like this. I ask a favor and suddenly we're arguing. Geez, forget it. I'll find someone else."

He started walking away.

"Sean?"

He stopped and looked back at me.

"Yeah, I'll invite Whitney to join us for lunch."

"Don't put yourself out."

"No, seriously, I'm sorry."

"Thanks. I owe you."

Again, I couldn't figure out why he owed me or why he cared so much about Whitney's happiness. Did he care about everyone assigned to his crew? Or was Whitney special?

He started to walk away again, stopped,

looked back at me. "You didn't tell Caitlin I was on probation."

He said it more like a statement than a question.

I shook my head. "No. How'd you know?"

"She didn't give me a hard time about it last night."

"She wouldn't —"

"She would. So, thanks. And don't forget to be nice to Whitney."

"Obviously you haven't noticed, but I do 'nice' really well."

He grinned. "I've noticed."

He strode away with a lazy walk that, contrary to the way it looked, actually covered a lot of ground quickly.

It was only when I headed to Splash that his words really struck me.

He'd noticed — noticed that I was nice. I didn't know why that knowledge made me feel really good. Maybe because I'd started noticing lately that he was nice, too.

* * *

Whitney, however, was still a challenge.

"Why do the kids even need to be in inner tubes?" she asked. "It's just a slide."

"Maybe they want to feel like it's a big-kid ride," I said as I held the tube for a toddler so she could climb in. She was the only one around at the moment because the park had just opened. Her mom was off to the side watching, which again made me wonder why I was even here.

"They're kids. Do you really think they notice?" Whitney was sitting on the edge of the pool again. "Maybe I'll suggest they do away with the inner tubes."

Like someone was going to listen to her suggestions. Honestly, why would she think anyone would care about what she had to say?

"If they did away with the tubes, we'd just be standing around watching kids slide," I said. I pushed the little girl down the slide and straightened, twisting one way, then the other, to get the kinks out of my back.

"And that's a problem because?" Whitney asked.

Okay, so most lifeguards just stood around watching people. And really, the inner tubes did seem like way more trouble than they were worth.

"You're thinking I'm right," Whitney said. "Admit it."

"Well, maybe."

She stood up. "I know. We've got a lull here, no day-care kiddos have arrived yet. So let's test my theory."

"Test?"

"Yeah. We'll slide down in a tube, then slide down without. We'll see which is the most fun."

"Uh, actually, we're not supposed —"

"Yeah, yeah, I know. We're not supposed to be about having any fun. We're just supposed to work, work, work — slave labor. Besides, who's gonna notice? Seriously?" She looked around. "The park just opened; there aren't that many people here yet."

She grabbed a tube from the mesh container. "Come on. I'll hold it while you get in. No one will know."

Well, Nick would know and a few people were in the distance, but they didn't look like they were paying any attention. And would Nick say anything? He didn't seem like a whistle-blower.

He was looking at us, grinning. "Go ahead, Robyn," he called up.

The water was so shallow that I figured the tube would stop me from plunging far enough down to get wet — so there would be no evidence of my transgression.

"For the good of the park," Whitney urged. "It's your duty."

What would it hurt? Truthfully, I missed playing in the park, so maybe this would satisfy those longings.

"Oh, okay," I finally said, giving in to the peer pressure.

I was only halfway on, not properly situated, when Whitney said, "Have fun!" and pushed me — really hard!

I went flying down the slide, screaming at the suddenness of it. I hit the cold water, dipped over, and landed facedown in the pool. I came up sputtering, and my gaze settled on a pair of firm, tanned calves — set right in front of me.

I lifted my gaze. The legs belonged to Sean. His arms were crossed over his chest as he stared down at me. Where had he come from? And how had he shown up so fast?

"What. Are. You. Doing?" he asked.

Getting. In. Trouble.

"I can't believe you were doing that," Sean said.

He'd led me over to that little table where we'd taken a break together the day before. Not that we were sitting, enjoying the park. Oh, no, we were standing with him hovering over me. When had he gotten so tall? So broad? So scary?

"You know the rules. No goofing around." His voice was firm. He was mad, really mad.

"Yeah, but see, Whitney had this theory that we didn't really need the inner tubes —"

He took off his sunglasses. I could see the disgust in his blue, blue eyes. "We paired her up with you —"

"We?"

"Yeah. TPTB."

"TPTB?" I was so lost.

"The Powers That Be. The guys in charge. They asked if anyone knew someone who was really dependable and I said you, because usually you are."

I knew I should have been flattered, that somewhere in his anger was a compliment. But dependable? I was, but suddenly that sounded so boring. Maybe that was part of the reason that I'd gone down the slide — because I never did anything I wasn't supposed to do and where was it getting me? Whitney wasn't doing anything she was supposed to do and she was still employed. Not only that, her supervisor was doing everything possible to keep her happy. What was up with that anyway?

Sean had to want her to be his girlfriend, but wasn't that against park rules? To date someone you were in charge of?

"You're the reason Caitlin doesn't get into any more trouble than she does," Sean continued.

Okay, I *was* the one who talked her out of trying to self-pierce her eyebrow — but I didn't think he knew about that. He did know about the time she wanted to dump bubble bath in the hot tub, and I convinced her it would be a bad idea — that we'd suffocate in bubbles.

"I mean, I thought you were incorruptible," he said.

"I went down a slide," I said, getting a little fed up with his attitude. "A little slide. It's not like I broke the law."

"You broke a park rule." He held up a finger. "And don't you dare say rules are meant to be broken."

"That's Caitlin, not me." She was always saying that.

He shook his head. "Look, just don't goof around anymore." He put his sunglasses back on. "We've got six day-care centers scheduled for field trips today, so stay alert. And don't forget to take Whitney with you for lunch."

"After what just happened? Are you serious?"

"Yeah, I'm serious."

"Are you going to talk to her about this incident? It was her idea."

"Ideas aren't against park rules. Going down the slides is."

Picky. Picky. If he hadn't shown up so fast, *she* would have been going down the slide.

So he wasn't going to say anything to her. Unfair!

He walked away and I strode back to Splash. Whitney was actually helping a boy get into the inner tube. When she gave him a little push, she looked at me and said, "He looked seriously mad."

"Thanks a lot for standing by me."

"We were just having fun."

"But we're supposed to be working."

"So what's your opinion on the tubes? Do they stay or go?"

Did she not get it at all?

"They stay. Why don't you go down there and help Nick?"

"He has less to do than you do."

"What does it matter? You're not doing anything anyway."

She pouted. I'd never seen an actual pout. She jutted out her lower lip. "Fine."

She hopped on the slide, slid down.

I looked around for Sean, expecting him to show up and yell at her — but he was nowhere to be seen. Or maybe he was hiding. Maybe he didn't want to have to get after her.

When she got to the bottom, she looked up at me. "The tubes definitely need to go!"

Something — or someone — needed to go. Her or me.

CHAPTER SIX

I wasn't going to invite Whitney to lunch. I really wasn't. I didn't care what Sean said.

But he was the one who came over to relieve us. I guess since he wasn't taking his lunch at the same time that we were, he had to find a lunch buddy for Whitney. I really didn't want to be it.

But he took off his sunglasses and stared at me with those amazing blue eyes of his. I stared back. He was bigger. And he was my boss.

What was the deal? Why did he care who she ate lunch with?

"Whitney's going to have lunch with us."

Caitlin was already in the lounging area at the wave pool when I arrived. I'd told Whitney to meet us there — which worked since she had to buy her lunch while I grabbed mine out of my locker. I wanted a couple of minutes to prepare Caitlin, to let her know that Sean wanted us to be nice to Whitney.

"That was his big, mysterious you-can't-be-here-while-I-talk-to-her moment?"

"Yeah."

"He can be such a jerk."

"No kidding."

It was weird. I felt disloyal to Sean — agreeing with Caitlin. But I always agreed with Caitlin. And right that moment, I did think that Sean was a jerk.

I was still stinging from his getting mad at me. It bothered me more than I'd realized at the time — not so much that I'd gotten into trouble, but that I'd somehow let Sean down. I didn't know why I wanted to impress him with my ability to be an exceptional employee, but I did.

And it totally wasn't fair that I'd gotten all the blame when it was Whitney's idea. He should have at least told her not to come up with any more ideas. Of course, that sounded ridiculous when I thought about it.

"So how long does it take to grab your lunch?" Caitlin asked.

"She doesn't bring her lunch. She had to get something from Scavenger's."

Scavenger's was a shack-looking building that served hot dogs, nachos, popcorn, candy, and anything else unhealthy. Although it was really a sturdy building, it looked like it would collapse at any moment, like it had survived a storm. It was all part of the island illusion.

"She buys her lunch every day?" Caitlin asked.

"Apparently."

"That gets expensive. Even with our employee discount. So if she can afford that, why's she working here?"

"You seem to forget. She's not actually *working*."

"Okay, then, why is she getting paid to be here?"

I shrugged. "She said her dad was making her. Let's just be nice to her and get this lunch over with."

I saw Whitney looking around. I stood up and waved. When she spotted me, I sat back down. Maybe she wouldn't come over. But I couldn't be that lucky. She started walking our way.

"She's kinda strutting over here like she thinks she owns the park," Caitlin said.

"Yeah, she really has this attitude. But be nice to her, because for some reason it's important to Sean."

"I'm not sure why that would make it matter to me."

"Come on, Caitlin. He's your brother."

"Oh, okay. Although I think that's a rumor — that he's actually my brother. I think my real brother was stolen at birth."

She'd told me that a hundred times. It was like her little joke, but I was starting to think that Sean really wasn't that bad. I wished I had a brother so I understood how the whole sibling thing was supposed to work.

Whitney walked past me, dropped her leather bag on the ground, and stretched out on the lounge chair beside mine. She didn't have her lunch with her, so I guess she'd eaten it at the food court. That would explain why it had taken her an exceptionally long time to join us.

"This is Caitlin," I said. "Sean's sister."

Whitney moved her sunglasses down her nose and peered over at Caitlin. Neither one said anything, like they were sizing each other up. It made me uncomfortable.

"Caitlin is a lifeguard at Tsunami," I felt a need to say, to fill the silence.

"That has to be boring," Whitney said.

"You're kidding, right?" Caitlin asked. "Do you not see the smorgasbord of hot guys around here?"

Caitlin was all talk. She'd probably picked up "smorgasbord of hot guys" from one of her teen mags.

"We've got some pretty hot guys where we work," Whitney said.

I know my jaw dropped. What alternate universe was she working in?

"Oh, yeah," Caitlin retorted. "Mini Falls really appeals to the hunks."

Whitney shoved her sunglasses back into place. She didn't say anything. Like she didn't see the point. Like she thought she'd won the argument or whatever was going on between them.

"Is that a Cartier watch?" Caitlin asked.

Whitney lifted her arm to look at her wrist like she just realized she had a watch on it. "Knockoff."

"And the Louis Vuitton bag?"

"Knockoff. I order from a designer knockoff website. I'll try to remember to get you the URL. No promises, though. I don't usually remember to do inconsequential things."

I so didn't get Whitney. It was like she didn't want us to like her.

"You know, you kinda remind me of someone," Caitlin said.

"I just have that kind of face."

"Maybe. So, do you have a boyfriend?"

Caitlin wasn't one to give up. I might be the good influence, but she was the one with determination. She was also nosy. She liked knowing things about people.

"What is this? An interrogation?" Whitney asked.

"Just trying to get to know you," Caitlin said. "After all, I know everything about Robyn. We don't know anything about you."

"You two are friends?" Whitney asked.

"Oh, yeah," Caitlin said. "Long time."

Whitney leaned up a bit so she could look directly at Caitlin. "So, why do you do all the talking?"

Caitlin shifted her attention to me. "I don't do all the talking."

"You do most of it." I shrugged. "But that's okay."

I could tell Caitlin was thinking lunch with Whitney was not going to become a routine for us, which sorta made me feel sorry for Whitney. That she seemed to have a knack for getting people to not like her. Well, except for Sean, of course. He seemed to think she was the greatest thing since the invention of the iPod.

"So what do you like to do for fun, Whitney?" I asked.

"Oh, you know? Shop."

Hence all the knockoffs.

I looked over at Caitlin. She faked a yawn. Yeah, Whitney was really making our lunchtime boring.

Caitlin leaned in. "Okay, check this out. See the guy standing at the edge of the waves?"

It was a lifeguard, holding his rescue tube. Not the guy she'd pointed out the day before. He had blond hair and looked really athletic.

"That's Tanner. I like him — a lot."

I could see why. He was cute. As though

he could feel our gazes on him, he looked over at us and grinned. He gave a little wave before turning his attention back to the people in the pool.

I released a tiny squeal, reached out, and tapped Caitlin's knee. "You go, girl!"

Grinning broadly, she nodded. "I know. He came over and talked to me before our shift started and then came back over on his morning break. It was awesome."

"You're not obsessed with guys, are you?" Whitney asked.

"Well, yeah, I am," Caitlin said. "It's the whole reason I'm working here. An abundance of boyfriend material."

Whitney looked at me. "You, too?"

I shook my head. "Sorta, but mostly for me it's money for a car. I really want to buy a car when I turn sixteen."

"What kind?" she asked, like she was really interested.

"Used."

She cringed. "OMG, why would you buy something that someone else has already owned? They could have barfed in it and you wouldn't know."

I didn't want that image in my head when I went car shopping. Why did she have to say that?

"Look, I need something cheap, okay?"

"Maybe Whitney can hook you up with a knockoff Ferrari," Caitlin said.

"Maybe I can," Whitney said.

I felt like I was sitting between two hissing cats. Maybe there was a reason Caitlin and I had always been a group of two. Maybe she didn't play well with others. Of course, Whitney was difficult to play with.

And me? I just couldn't wait for lunch to be over.

I'd never been very good at lying. Maybe it was because when I was a kid, my mom told me that my eyes turned purple when I lied — they didn't, of course, but when you're a kid you believe in a lot of things that aren't true. Like the tooth fairy.

So when I was a kid, I'd always close my eyes when I lied, so Mom wouldn't see them turning purple. *Duh?!?* I know. Eventually I figured out that closing my eyes gave it away.

Anyway, I still have this thing about thinking people can look at me and tell when I'm lying. But I gave it my best shot. After lunch I told Whitney that I was going to the first-aid station for some Tylenol because I was getting a headache.

Actually, it wasn't too much of a lie. Listening to her and Caitlin had made my head start to throb. So I did stop by the first-aid station for some Tylenol — as a preventative measure.

Then, even though it was going to make me late returning to my post, I walked slowly through Mini Falls trying to find Sean. I really needed to talk with him. And I figured he would have left Splash when Whitney showed up, because really two of us weren't needed there. Sometimes I felt like I was babysitting her as much as I was the kids coming through our area.

I hadn't signed up for this.

I finally spotted Sean at the petting tank. That was the one awesome thing about Mini Falls. It had two dolphins that just swam around, and people could go up and pet them. An employee stood watch, of course, to make sure that no one hurt the animals. Why anyone would try to hurt them was beyond me, but some people can't be trusted to be decent. Sad but true.

Anyway, I thought the petting tank was one of the coolest things about the water park.

Sean was the only employee around, so I figured he was giving the tank attendant a break. Sean was explaining about the dolphins, demonstrating how to touch them, and encouraging a young girl not to be afraid. It hadn't occurred to me that he needed to know everything about all the different positions so he could fill in for various workers. I found myself being impressed again.

It really was a shame that he was Caitlin's brother, and my supervisor. And a jerk for chewing me out earlier over something that wasn't my fault —

He looked up, furrowed his brow. "Hey, aren't you supposed to be back at work?"

"Yeah, but I needed to talk to you."

"Okay. Hold on." As soon as the little girl had petted the dolphin and rushed off, Sean motioned me over. "What's up?"

"This whole Whitney thing —"

"Yeah, look, I'm sorry about that."

Before I could ask about what exactly, he said, "Mr. T told me that Whitney had that idea about getting rid of the tubes. He liked it, so they took them away while y'all were at lunch."

Was that the reason Whitney was late in joining Caitlin and me for lunch? Because she was talking to the manager? How many new employees went to talk with the general manager? How bold could she get?

And hadn't I told him it was Whitney's idea? Didn't he even listen to anything I said?

"So what do we do now?" I asked.

"Just stand around, hold your rescue tubes, and watch the kids."

"Oh." Wasn't as much work, but would probably be more boring. I looked at him. "Oh, okay, great."

"Yeah, great," he muttered. "Anyway, thanks for being nice to Whitney."

"You know, it really bugs me when you thank me for being what I have no control over — I mean, being nice is what I do."

He grinned. "Which is why I've never been able to understand you hanging out with Caitlin."

"She's nice, too."

"Maybe, but I don't see it. How did she and Whitney get along?"

"Uh, honestly? Not great. Which is what I wanted to talk to you about. I'm not sure Whitney having lunch with us is going to work."

"Make it work, will you? Whitney really likes you."

I stared at him. "Does she not understand the definition of *like*?"

He grinned. "Come on, she's really not that bad."

"You keep saying that."

"What's she done that's so awful?"

I reached into the tank and patted a dolphin as it swam by. It felt so slick. The other dolphin came over, rose up out of the water, and made a gawking noise. I rubbed it, too.

I couldn't think of anything that Whitney had done that was really and truly awful. It was painful to admit, but I said, "She's irritating. But I guess she hasn't done anything *awful*."

"There you go."

He reached in to pet the dolphin. Our fingers brushed. My reaction was weird. It felt like electricity had shot through me. He seemed stunned as well, because he moved back quickly.

"Anyway," he said, adjusting his visor. "You better get back to your post."

"Right." I backed up a step. Seemed like I needed to say something else, but I couldn't think of what it was.

I spun on my heel and headed back to Splash. What was wrong with me? Why did I want to stay by the pet tank so badly?

Not because the dolphins were there.

But because Sean was.

CHAPTER SEVEN

Saturday, Memorial Day weekend, the parking lot was almost full by the time we arrived for work. People were lined up with beach bags and ice coolers. And little kids. Lots and lots of little kids.

It was going to be a very busy day. I probably wouldn't even have time to notice how lazy Whitney was.

As employees, we got front-of-the-line privileges. Well, actually, we had a special entrance, a gate off to the side where we swiped our employee IDs. The gate clicked open and in we went, saying hi to the guard on the other side.

After changing into our uniforms in the employee locker room, I promised Caitlin I'd see her at lunch and headed to Splash. Nick was already there waiting. Whitney was oddly, or maybe not so oddly, absent.

Maybe she'd convinced her dad that he didn't want her to work. Or maybe she'd gotten fired. Who knew with her? And here I was all prepared to be nice.

The area filled up pretty quickly once the park actually opened. Little kids yelling and screaming and rushing down the slide, throwing water on me. Wild and crazy. I really wished I could be doing my own playing.

About half an hour into my shift, Whitney strolled over.

"It's insane around here," she said, like maybe I hadn't noticed.

"You wanna help?"

"Not really." She crossed her arms over her chest. "There's no place that I can sit without getting splashed. Can't you make them go away?"

I stared at her openmouthed. "You're not serious."

"Dead."

"Why don't you go sit in the kiddie pavilion or, I don't know — walk around. It's not like you're really helping here."

"This is my assignment."

A little girl almost tumbled. I caught her before she smashed her chin on the edge of the slide. "Okay, kids, calm down!"

Where was her mother?

"Like they're going to listen to you," Whitney said.

"You wanna try?"

She shook her head. "Nah. Not worth the energy." She glanced around. "You know, without the tubes we really don't have much to do over here. Getting rid of them might not have been one of my brightest ideas."

"What do you care? You weren't doing anything anyway."

"But you were. And it was so much fun to watch you work."

I sighed. She was really annoying. I returned to watching the kids. They seemed okay with the slide only, didn't even seem to notice that the tubes were gone. Of course, maybe this was their first time here, and they didn't know better.

I saw Sean striding through, making his rounds. He cut a sharp corner, coming toward us. I wondered if maybe he'd finally — at last — noticed that Whitney was pretty much useless as an employee.

"Hey, Robyn," he said when he got close. "I was wondering if you could do us a favor."

How many favors was he going to ask for? Did I have "favor-giver" tattooed across my forehead? On the other hand, perfect employees moved up the ranks, right? So, I said, "Sure."

"Lisa is the supervisor for parties and entertainment. Someone overbooked. We've got, like, eight parties coming in at the kiddie pavilion, so could you go help her out?"

Something to do besides stand around? I couldn't say yes fast enough, mostly because before I could say anything, Whitney said, "I'm most excellent with giving parties. I can do it."

I was shocked that she'd volunteer to do *anything*.

"Yeah, but I already asked Robyn."

I wanted to hug him for not changing his mind about me. "Where do I go? The pavilion?" I asked.

"Yep. Just tell Lisa I sent you."

"Thanks."

I hurried off before Whitney cast her spell over him and made him forget that he'd asked me first. She had some sort of control over him, making him think she was nice, letting her get away with things he scolded me for.

Lisa was hard to miss. She was almost six feet tall. She was wearing red shorts and the familiar white polo shirt. She smiled broadly as I approached.

"Great!" she said. "You must be Robyn. Sean said he'd send you over."

How had he known I'd come? Maybe he'd only made it *sound* like he was asking. Maybe when it came right down to it, he was going to order me to come over here. It didn't matter. I was away from Whitney.

"So what do you need me to do?" I asked.

"We've got about an hour before the first party arrives. To start with, we need a lot of balloons. I've put a reserved sign with the party's name and number on each table. You just tie that many balloons to the ring at the end of the table. Can you do it?"

"Oh, yeah."

"Wonderful. Sean said you were his go-to girl."

Before I could ask her what that meant, she was hurrying off to see about something else. As I walked over to the helium tank, I thought about Sean saying positive things about me, asking me — me, not Whitney — to help out during a crisis. Maybe he was beginning to realize that I was nice. Made sense, since I was starting to think he was nice.

I reached the tank and saw the box of balloons resting beside it. I inserted the first balloon on the nozzle, blew it up, tied it off, and wrapped the end of the ribbon around a nearby chair. I reached for another —

"Oh, good, more helpers," Lisa shouted.

I looked over. It was Sean and Whitney. Sean stopped and talked with Lisa while Whitney walked over to me.

"Who's watching Splash with Nick?" I asked.

"Sean found someone. I wanted to help. I love doing parties."

I couldn't believe it. How had she wrapped him around her finger like that? He had to have a crush on her, had to want her to be his girlfriend. But why say I was his go-to girl? And why did I want so badly to be his go-to girl?

"You do realize we're not actually invited to the party. We're just supposed to help."

"Oh, sure."

"Hey, Whitney, you want to help me put out the party favors?" Lisa asked.

"Oh, yeah. I love giving gifts."

She said it like the gifts were from her personally.

Smiling, Sean came over. "I'm pretty fast at doing balloons. Why don't I blow them up, you tie them off?"

I thought about how many we had to get done. "Sure."

I moved aside. He grabbed a balloon, but before he attached it, he put the hose in his mouth, swallowed a breath —

"Shouldn't take us long," he said in a high-pitched squeaky voice that made me burst out laughing. He grinned broadly. "Want a hit?"

Laughing even harder, I shook my head. "I get in trouble for sliding down a slide in an inner tube and you play with helium?"

He stopped grinning. "Oh, man, what was I thinking?"

He still sounded like a chipmunk — if chipmunks could talk.

"I won't tell," I promised.

It was so funny, so strange, seeing him not so serious. He was the one who was always looking out for Caitlin. Both their parents worked, and he'd taken care of her after they decided he was old enough. I never realized that he could actually be fun, had never stopped to think how much responsibility he shouldered.

He blew up a balloon, handed it off to me.

"So, uh." How did I say this? "So you decided to let Whitney help, too?"

"Yeah, she really wanted to. Was practically begging." He sounded normal again, his voice deep, which made me smile. "I don't get girls and parties."

"Shouldn't you be supervising?" I asked.

"Someone's covering. Newbie supervisor. I go where I'm told." He nodded toward someone. "Hey, Jake."

It was the ice-cream guy. He was even cuter up close, with dark, serious eyes.

"Got the ice cream," he said, pointing toward a silver cart on wheels.

"Talk to Lisa. This is her gig," Sean told him.

"Will do." He walked away.

"So we give the partygoers ice cream?" I asked.

"We do everything except the cake. They bring that."

"Makes it easy on us, I guess."

He laughed. "Yeah, right."

"Okay, okay, y'all need to work harder," Whitney said, taking a group of the balloons. "Front gate just radioed Lisa and the first group is on its way in."

I didn't miss the fact that we — not Whitney — needed to work harder. I didn't know how we managed to do it, but we had all the balloons in place by the time the first group joined us. Twenty kids around the age of eight were screaming, laughing, and running around.

And that was just the first group. By the time all eight groups arrived, it was madness. But what really surprised me was what Sean did with the balloons. Not the ones he'd blown up using the helium. But the ones he was using to make balloon animals. He went from table to table, entertaining the kids, creating fish, ducks, crocodiles. I was pretty impressed.

Jake was scooping out ice cream. Whitney was taking pictures of people, borrowing their cameras, making sure everyone was in the party picture, making a big production out of posing the group. Lisa was making sure everyone had everything they needed. And me?

I was trash girl. Sounds a little like a superhero, but I rolled a big trash container around and put the discarded gift wrap, used paper plates, empty cups, and anything else that looked like garbage into the can. We only had to watch the groups for an hour or so. Then they were on their own.

I was working at a table, clearing away the debris when I felt a tap on my shoulder. I turned around. Sean was holding a balloon dolphin out to me.

"Thanks for helping today," he said.

I took it from him. "Thanks. That was nice of you."

Sean smiled at me. "Maybe you haven't noticed but I do 'nice' really well!."

Hadn't I said practically the same thing to him yesterday? And okay, I had started to notice, but it made me feel funny to admit it. I'd spent so much of my life believing he was a jerk. What would Caitlin say if I told her that I thought her brother was nice?

Caitlin!

I looked at my watch. "Oh, my gosh! I missed lunch with Caitlin."

"She'll survive," Sean said.

I wasn't so sure.

"Hey, guys, let's finish cleaning up real quick so we can grab something to eat. We have a group of thirty six-year-olds coming at two," Lisa said. "It's going to be wild."

"You didn't even let me know," Caitlin said.

She was sitting on the lifeguard platform, staring at the pool. The waves were calm. In a little bit, they'd sound the alarm and the pool would shift into Tsunami mode, creating its eight-foot waves.

"I didn't know I'd be there that long," I said, staring up at her. My neck was starting to ache. "We just got busy and time flew."

"I had to eat alone. It made me look like a total loser. How can I impress Tanner if it looks like no one wants to hang out with me?"

What could I say to that? I knew Caitlin didn't like doing things by herself.

"I'm sure no one noticed," I said, trying to appease her.

"What are you doing hanging out with my brother and Whitney anyway?" she asked.

"We weren't hanging out — we were working the birthday parties." I glanced at my watch. Sean had told us we could all eat at the food court, that management would treat us to lunch. Even though I'd brought a sandwich, I was really in the mood for a burger, so I wanted to get to the food court. "I've got to go get something to eat. I'll see you after work."

The alarm sounded, signaling that the large waves were about to start up.

"Yeah. All right. Later," she said.

I wanted to believe she was distracted watching the swimmers, making sure they were all safe. I didn't like Caitlin being upset with me, but it really hadn't been my fault. I hadn't considered that when you're working, a lot of things happen that you have no control over — that you have to put the job first. Unless you're Whitney, of course.

But I didn't want to be Whitney. I liked being Sean's go-to girl. I couldn't tell Caitlin that, though. She wouldn't understand that

I was starting to like her brother — as a person. That I thought he was nice. That I was impressed with how hard he worked, everything he knew, everything he did.

I wandered over to the food court, knowing that I wouldn't have much time to eat — might not even have time to order anything. So many people were standing in line at Scavenger's that I decided I'd just grab my lunch out of my locker.

Before I could turn to head back to my locker, I saw Sean stand up and wave at me. He was at a table with Whitney and Jake.

"Went ahead and ordered you a burger," Sean said when I got there.

"Oh, geez, thanks, but —"

"I know. Meat, cheese, mustard only."

"How did you know?"

"Come on, Robyn. You practically live at our house."

He suddenly seemed embarrassed. Me, I was stunned that he'd noticed my eating habits. Granted, he'd been right about the ice cream. His mom did keep a carton with my name on it in their freezer. But how I liked my burger? We didn't have burgers that often. When had he noticed?

I sat down and unwrapped it. Everyone else was almost finished eating.

"We didn't think you'd have much time," Whitney said, as though she was the one responsible for making sure I had food.

"Where's Lisa?" I asked, just before biting into my burger.

"She wanted to get back to start setting up for the next set of parties," Sean said.

"Is it just me or were these parties boring?" Whitney asked.

"They were kids' parties," I told her. How exciting could they be?

"Still. Balloon animals. That's so . . ."

While she was trying to think of a word that I figured wouldn't be flattering, I said, "I thought they were great." I turned to Sean. "I didn't even know you could do that."

He grinned. "There's a bunch of videos out on the Internet. You can pretty much learn anything out there."

"We should do face painting," Whitney said.

"It'd just come off when they went into the water," I said.

"I guess." She sighed. "These little birthday parties put me in the mood to have a real party."

"Do they ever do anything here after the park closes?" Jake asked. "You know — can you rent it out or anything?"

She smiled at him. "Yeah, I'm pretty sure you can. Wouldn't that be great — to have a party here?"

"Yeah, it would. You know, when I applied to work here, scooping ice cream wasn't exactly what I had in mind," Jake said.

Was anyone satisfied with their assignment? Caitlin was happy, I guess. I hadn't really asked her. Now that she was actually doing it, maybe it wasn't as great as it seemed.

"Well, we'd better head back," Sean said.

"I gotta go refill the ice-cream tubs. I'll meet you at the kiddie pavilion," Jake said, and walked off in the opposite direction that we'd be heading.

"You know if I see one more kid unwrap a Transformer —" Whitney began.

"Hey, come on. They're awesome," Sean said.

"I guess you had some."

"Oh, yeah."

"But he never took them out of the box," I said.

"They stay more valuable that way."

"But you can't transform them! So why get them?"

"I collect them."

"You two sure know a lot about each other," Whitney said.

It was weird to realize that we really did.

"Did you two date or something?" she asked.

"No!" we both said at the same time.

"Absolutely not," I added.

Sean's face was turning red. I could feel the heat on my cheeks.

"Time to get back to work," he repeated.

He didn't wait for us. Just picked up his trash and carted it to the trash can.

"Very interesting," Whitney murmured.

"You must be easily bored," I told her — if she found Sean and me interesting.

"I am," she said grinning. "I really don't want to do another set of parties."

"Too bad. You asked for it," I reminded her as I gathered up my trash and dumped it into the trash can.

"Yeah, I guess."

We were walking back when she suddenly said, "What do you think of Jake?"

"He's cute. Why?"

"I don't know."

"Do you like him?"

She shrugged. "I don't really know him. It just seems like he looks at me a lot."

"Maybe *he* likes *you*."

"Yeah, right."

Okay, that was a complete turnaround from a similar conversation we'd had where she agreed that he thought she was cute. Was she starting to let her guard down, starting to trust me? Or was she just messing with me?

"What? You don't think a guy could like you?" I asked.

"I don't know if I want a guy to like me."

If we didn't need to get back to the kiddie pavilion as quickly as possible, I would have stopped and stared at her. "Why not?"

She looked around as though someone might hear us. Then she shook her head. "Nothing."

"Whitney, you can tell me."

"Oh, sure. And then you'll go tell everyone else. I know you don't like me. No one likes me."

"I like you." *Some*, I added silently. "After all, you are adorable."

She grinned. "Yeah, I guess I am. And you won't tell anyone?"

I'd never not told Caitlin something. It felt like a betrayal. But still, I heard myself say, "I promise."

She stopped walking. So did I.

"I've never had a boyfriend." She groaned. "Who am I kidding? I've never even had a date."

"That's not so awful. Neither have I. Had a boyfriend, I mean. Or a date."

"I really thought — you and Sean."

"Why would you think that?"

"I don't know. Y'all just seem to have this connection."

"I spend a lot of time at his house and do things with his family — because of Caitlin, but that's all."

"If you say so."

"Believe me, Sean and me, no way." But even as I said it, I didn't sound very convincing. Was I starting to think of him differently?

"Whatever," Whitney said. "My problem is my dad. He is, like, so superprotective. I'm afraid he'd make any guy who was interested fill out an application, go through a security check, and pee in a bottle so he could do a drug test."

"No way!" I said, laughing. We'd had to do a drug test to get this job. I'd been a little insulted that it was assumed I might be taking drugs. On the other hand, I figured they couldn't afford to take a chance that someone would be high around water.

"Way. It's kinda sad really."

"It's almost pathetic." I wondered if my dad had hung around if he would have been protective, if he would have interrogated any potential boyfriends. And while I did agree that her dad was extreme, in a way, it was sort of nice that he paid that much attention.

"Anyway," she said. "I'm sure I can get a boyfriend. I just have to set my mind to it."

"Because you can have anything you want?"

"That's right."

But I was beginning to think maybe she couldn't. And she knew it.

CHAPTER EIGHT

"So how was work?" Mom asked me later when I walked into the kitchen after Sean had dropped me off. She was at the counter chopping a tomato.

An empty jar of spaghetti sauce was on the counter — its former contents probably in the microwave — and a pot of noodles was on the stove. Mom wasn't exactly a gourmet chef.

"It was insane. We had soooo many people."

"That's great," she said. "Job security."

"No kidding." But it was also exhausting.

As soon as I finished eating, I planned to crash.

"Will you grab the salad out of the fridge?" Mom asked.

Which meant grabbing a plastic bag of shredded lettuce. I poured some into bowls and Mom scraped the chopped tomato on top. I snatched up the bottle of Italian dressing, while Mom got the bowl of sauce out of the microwave and some garlic bread out of the oven.

When we had everything ready, we sat at the counter to eat. We weren't big on eating at the table because that just meant something else to wipe down when we were finished. So we usually just ate in the kitchen.

Mom and I looked a lot alike. She had brown eyes and brown hair that brushed her shoulders. I had a few freckles across my nose. Mom didn't have any but then she pretty much avoided the sun as much as possible. She had this thing about getting skin cancer. Not that I blamed her. It was a problem — which was the reason I slathered on sunblock several times during the day.

"So tell me about your insane day," she said. "It has to be more entertaining than my battle with dust bunnies."

That was Mom's way of saying she'd spent the day cleaning the house — which made me really grateful that I'd had to work. Scrubbing toilets was so not my idea of fun.

I told Mom about the birthday parties. How the afternoon had been even crazier than the morning. Someone had made a mistake and written down the wrong age of the birthday boy.

"We thought we were hosting a party for a six-year-old," I said. "And he was sixteen!"

Mom laughed. "He must have liked being in the kiddie area."

"Oh, yeah. With balloon animals? I don't think so. They found an available cabana and moved the party over there, gave them discounts to the souvenir shops."

"Sounds like someone was thinking outside the box."

Whitney. She suggested moving them to a cabana. We rented the cabanas out to guests and they got their own personal assistant who ran around getting things for them.

"We also had a party show up that hadn't been written down. We scrambled to make a place for them. The mom was so upset," I said, "you'd have thought we did it on purpose."

"People get like that," Mom said. "I think it's great that you're working so young. Gives you a chance to see that there are all kinds of people in the world."

"Speaking of all kinds of people — there's this one girl and I can't decide if I like her." Mom and I hadn't really had a chance to talk much since I started work, mostly because I was so tired when I got home that all I wanted to do was relax. Even though I was more tired tonight, I also needed to talk, so I told her about Whitney.

"Sometimes she seems nice, seems like she wants to be friends — and then other times" — I growled — "she's so annoying."

"Maybe she's just not comfortable in the situation, doesn't really know how to act. You said her father's making her work?"

"Yeah."

"What does that mean exactly? Why is he doing that?"

I put my elbow on the table, and my chin in my palm. "I don't know. I didn't ask, but it's weird. I mean everything about her looks . . . well, rich. It's hard to explain. So maybe she just needs money to buy all the stuff she buys."

"Or maybe she is rich and he's trying to teach her the value of a dollar."

I twirled my fork in the middle of the noodles. I wasn't really hungry.

"Caitlin got mad at me because I didn't have lunch with her."

She hadn't said much on the ride home, which was weird because she usually talked about all the different people she'd seen at the pool — some of the craziness that goes on. She couldn't talk about Tanner, of course, because Sean was in the car and he'd give her a hard time if she talked about a guy. Or, at least, we thought he would. I was beginning to wonder if maybe Caitlin didn't know her brother as well as I did.

"You can't do everything together," Mom said.

"Yeah, but we always have. I just couldn't get to lunch because of helping out with the parties."

"She should understand that."

But I wasn't sure she had. As soon as I finished helping Mom clean up the dishes, I was going to call Caitlin. Make sure we were okay.

"Actually, I think it's good that you do some things without the other. You two have always had only each other — you need to expand your horizons."

I felt a lecture coming on. Mom worried that I was too shy, that I didn't know enough people. She was always prodding me to "Get out there! Experience life!" She'd been thrilled that I wanted to work this summer. Still, I didn't want to discuss my limited social life.

After I helped Mom clean up, I went to my bedroom and called Caitlin.

"Sorry about the mix-up at lunch. I really didn't do it on purpose," I told her.

"I know. Sean was telling Mom and Dad about all the party craziness during dinner."

Weird that we'd been having the same conversation in two different houses.

"So I know it was just too insane for you to get away. Sorry if I overreacted. But since we started working, it's like the only time I really see you is while we're in the car or during lunch. I mean, I'd hoped we'd be working in the same area, that we'd be spending time together — just working instead of playing. You know?"

"Yeah, I know."

"I've actually been thinking about asking if I could transfer to Splash. How sick is that?"

"Pretty sick. You really don't want to do that."

"You're right. If I moved, then I'd never see Tanner."

"Did he talk to you again today?"

"Oh, yeah, he always comes over and asks how I'm doing, but that's about it — mostly because I'm usually on duty at the time so we could get into trouble if we're caught yammering instead of 'being watchful' out there."

"Listen, if you can change your lunchtime so it matches his instead of mine, don't worry about me."

"You're such a great friend, Robyn."

"I try." And who knew? There might come a time when I wanted to change *my* lunchtime.

"So are you going with us to see the fireworks?" she asked.

Every year, the city put on a huge fireworks display for Memorial Day as a tribute to the troops. The high school band would play and the fireworks were choreographed to patriotic tunes. It didn't start until nine thirty and since the water park closed at eight we'd have plenty of time to get there.

"You bet. Don't I always?"

She laughed. "Yeah, some things never change."

But I had a feeling that wasn't going to be true for much longer. Seemed like some things were changing already. Maybe she just hadn't really noticed yet.

CHAPTER NINE

"This is going to be so much fun!" Caitlin said.

It was Monday evening, Memorial Day. We'd finished with work. The day had been more insane than I'd ever imagined it could be. Thousands and thousands of people had descended on the water park. I was so glad that we'd be doing something tonight that would be calm. Instead of having Sean take me home and then have to come back by to get me, I'd packed some extra clothes that morning so that I could change at Caitlin's. Her house was practically my house and vice versa.

We'd both taken quick showers, washed our hair. She was fluffing hers up, using some kind of gel or something to make it look windblown. I was wearing mine loose.

"Did you want to wear one of my headbands?" she asked.

She had several. They were all sparkly. And I'm just not really sparkly.

"No thanks."

Caitlin was wearing shorts and a T-shirt with sequins on it that spelled out PRINCESS. It was part of a set that Sean had given her for her birthday. The other two read QUEEN and DIVA. He was always buying her things that indicated he thought she was spoiled. Maybe she was. But then he probably was, too.

I was wearing a red tank top, denim shorts, and sandals. I fastened a seashell choker around my neck. I'd bought it in one of the Paradise Falls gift shops last year. It's a little embarrassing to admit, but Paradise Falls was the closest I'd come to going to a beach. It was one of those things that I wanted to do someday.

Maybe that was one of the reasons that I really enjoyed Paradise Falls. Even though it was all pretend, it was like being on a tropical island away from it all. And sometimes I just wanted to be away from it all.

"Oh, uh, listen, I should probably tell you that I invited Tanner to join us," Caitlin said.

I caught her gaze in the mirror. She was standing behind me looking guilty. I slowly turned around.

Before I could say anything, she shrugged. "He might not come. He probably won't. I mean, I just told him that we were going to be at the baseball field, you know, in case he wanted to come watch the fireworks. Maybe we'd see each other."

"What am I supposed to do if he shows up?"

"What do you mean?"

"Well, won't it be a little awkward?" *Two is company, three is a crowd? That sort of thing?*

"No, absolutely not. I just wanted to spend a little time with him. Get to know him better. This way, there's no pressure. Just friends having fun, and who knows? Maybe we'll get to know each other well enough that he might ask me out."

But I couldn't help but think that if he was there, I would really be alone. Caitlin would be giving all her attention to him. And Sean always went with us, but he never hung around with us. He usually ran into friends and would go off with them, and we'd always meet back up after the fireworks.

I guess what really surprised me was how bold Caitlin was being this summer — trying to get a boyfriend. Or a date. Or at least that first kiss.

Me, I figured it would all happen when it would happen. I couldn't force it.

Of course, Caitlin was in an area where there were a lot more guys — both lifeguards and guests. Me, kid city. Except for Nick. But he hadn't really shown any interest in me. We just rotated our positions around the slide and when he and I were at the top together, he didn't have much to say. Then there was Jake, but I really thought he was interested in Whitney.

"Anyway, I just wanted you to know so you wouldn't do that deer-in-the-headlights thing you do," Caitlin said.

"I don't do that."

"Sure you do," she said. "When something happens that you're not expecting, your eyes get really big and round. Like someone jumped out and said 'surprise!'"

"Great, Caitlin, thanks a lot. Now I'm going to worry that I have bug eyes."

She laughed. "Don't be silly. It's cute, really. Even Sean thinks so."

"You and Sean talk about my bug eyes?" I was amazed they'd talked about anything at all, but especially me.

"No, of course not. And they're not bug eyes. They just get big and round."

Sounded like bug eyes to me. I swung around and looked in the mirror. My eyes were brown. A deep brown. Like chocolate. When I'd gotten my restricted driver's license I'd asked the clerk to say my eyes were chocolate brown — but all she put was brown. So boring.

Big, round, brown, and boring.

"What are you doing?" she asked.

"Worrying about my big eyes."

"Well, don't. Everyone looks surprised when they're surprised. I just told you so you *wouldn't* look or be surprised. I want Tanner to think it's no big deal — having a guy meet up with me. And I'm nervous about tonight, okay?"

I turned back around. Caitlin wasn't usually a babbler. Her brow was furrowed. Maybe my eyes widened when I was surprised, but hers narrowed when she was worried.

"I really like him. I want him to think we're cool," she said. "If he even shows up."

A loud bang rattled the door. We both screeched. I figured my eyes got big, too.

"I'm leaving," Sean called out.

"Wait! We're not ready," Caitlin yelled.

"Too bad."

"He has no patience," Caitlin growled, grabbing her tote bag.

I snatched up my mine. I'd brought a quilt that my grandma had made. "Well, we were taking a long time."

"I wanted to be perfect."

"You are."

She opened the door. "You are, too. We both are."

It was odd to see Caitlin nervous.

When we got to the ballpark, Tanner was already there, waiting at the entrance. Caitlin immediately skipped to his side, leaving Sean and me to catch up.

It was strange. Until that moment I hadn't realized that it might look like Sean and I were together.

I'd done lots of things with Caitlin's family. Sean was usually there. Caitlin was always there. Sometimes it was the three of us. Mostly it was two of us: Caitlin and me. It had never been just Sean and me.

Sean and Tanner did a guy kind of greeting. I figured they knew each other. Made sense. All of us working at the park together. On the other hand, there were so many employees that it was hard to get to know everyone.

"This is Robyn," Caitlin said, indicating me. "My best friend."

"I've seen y'all at the park together," Tanner said. "And that other girl — what's her name?"

"Whitney," Sean said before either Caitlin or I could respond.

"Oh, yeah."

It sounded like he knew her but she

hadn't made much of an impression on him. Hard to believe.

"We better find a place," Caitlin said, "before all the good spots are taken."

"I told Whitney we'd meet her here," Sean said.

"Whitney's coming?" I asked, then blinked my eyes several times to keep them from looking big — anything not to look surprised. On the other hand, I *was* surprised.

"Yeah, she didn't have anything to do tonight. I figured you wouldn't mind," he said.

Okay, now I really was going to be the odd person out.

"We don't mind," Caitlin said.

I really struggled not to look surprised at that comment. She didn't even like Whitney.

"Here," Caitlin said, tugging the bag holding the quilt from my grasp. "Tanner and I will go find a spot on the knoll behind third base while y'all wait for Whitney."

I was used to Caitlin deciding what we were going to do, used to her not waiting for me to voice any objections, but waiting with Sean while he waited for Whitney, why would she think I'd want to do that? But with her already leaving with Tanner, I didn't know how to make a graceful exit.

So I stood there waiting.

"What's with all the eye blinking?" Sean asked. He was dressed in his usual black: black jeans, black T-shirt.

"What? Oh." I shook my head. "Something Caitlin said."

He chuckled. "She said something to make you blink your eyes? That makes no sense."

"She said that when I'm surprised, my eyes get big and round."

"Everyone's do. It's a reflex."

"Yeah, but now I'm thinking about it."

"So think about something else. Besides, guys like big eyes."

"They do?"

"Oh, yeah. Totally."

It was strange to realize that he was trying to make me feel better or make me feel more comfortable or something.

"Have you ever noticed the girl who works the ticket booth at the water park?" he asked. "All squinty. I can't even figure out what color her eyes are. Yours? No question. Brown."

He noticed my eyes? Well, I guess they were hard to miss. And I had noticed his. A long time ago.

He glanced around, obviously looking for Whitney, wanting to make sure he didn't miss her. Why was I even still here? All I had to do was say that I was going to go on in. Then I could find Caitlin and feel awkward around her and Tanner, which would probably be worse since I didn't even know Tanner. *Maybe I should just call my mom and ask her to come get me. Tell her I have a headache or something.*

"Let me ask you something," Sean finally said.

"Sure."

"Is it driving Caitie crazy trying to figure out who the new cute babe at the park is?"

"How did you know —" And then it dawned on me. I felt my eyes widen, and I didn't care. "You sneak!"

He laughed. "Hey, it's only fair. If she wasn't always eavesdropping, I wouldn't have to do it. She is so nosy."

I couldn't believe he'd told me. It was like a true confession or something. "So there is no cutie?" I asked.

He shrugged. "There are lots of cute babes."

"But not one in particular?"

"Nope. I was talking to one of my buds, knew she was outside my room, so I started making stuff up. I do it all the time when I know she's listening. Come on, admit it, she deserves it."

I wasn't going to admit it. She was my friend. My friend who wasn't here at the park entrance with me. So what was I doing? Flirting with her brother? No, I was just talking with him.

"Hey, guys!" Whitney called out as she walked quickly toward us. She was wearing a white camisole, jeans, and sandals with a jeweled T-strap that I thought Caitlin would probably kill for. Whitney had a matching tote bag slung over her shoulder.

Then, as though she realized that she was acting too excited about being here, she slowed down and stopped smiling. "Wow. This is such a little park."

She said it like it was an insult to be a small park, like it was suddenly beneath her to be here.

"Minor league teams play here," Sean said, "but the fireworks are spectacular."

He led the way through the gate and turnstile. It was already pretty crowded, with most of the seats in the bleachers filled. We walked along the path that ran around the top of the seating section.

"So where's your partner in crime?" Whitney asked.

"What?" I asked.

"You know. Caitlin."

"Oh, she went ahead to save us a place. Tanner is here, too."

"Really?" Her eyes widened slightly. A surprised look wasn't as bad as I thought. "That's the guy who stands at the edge of the water looking bored, right?"

"Yeah."

"So is it a date?"

"No, not really. We're just all hanging out together."

We'd gotten to the knoll behind third base. Sean started walking down the steps.

"We're sitting on grass?" Whitney asked.

"Yeah, it's more fun," I said.

"It's where the bugs are."

"It's not like we're in the woods. And we brought a quilt."

Caitlin stood up and started waving. And I suddenly wondered why I was standing here trying to convince Whitney that she wanted to sit with us. Sean invited her. Shouldn't he be the one calming her fears about bugs?

"Sit where you want," I said, getting tired of having to be nice, being constantly surprised by things, and feeling like my life was suddenly out of control. What was supposed to have been a fun, relaxing evening watching fireworks was suddenly awkward and included people I didn't know, people I wasn't sure that I wanted to know.

I heard the click of heels on the cement steps and knew Whitney was following me. She probably didn't want to be sitting alone any more than I did. And that made me feel guilty for being impatient.

Sean was standing by the quilt, waiting for us. Correction, waiting for Whitney. When I got there, I sat beside Caitlin. Tanner was on the other side of her. Whitney sat beside me and Sean sat beside her.

So it was really obvious that I was the only one here without a guy.

Were fireworks worth this embarrassment?

If I'd known earlier that Caitlin had invited Tanner and Sean had invited

Whitney, I would have invited someone, too. Nick, maybe. Or Jake even. He was cute. Then I wouldn't be sitting here feeling like a total loser.

"Oh, my gosh, are those Ferragamos?" Caitlin asked after Whitney turned slightly, stretched out her legs, and crossed her feet at the ankles.

"Knockoffs," Whitney said like she was totally bored.

"I love those shoes. Did you get them at that website you were telling me about?"

"No, someplace else."

"Where?"

"If I told you, I'd have to kill you."

Caitlin rolled her eyes. "Come on, Whitney. I love flashy stuff."

"I really can't remember."

Sean leaned over and said something to Tanner, who shook his head and smiled. They were probably ready to barf with all the shoe talk. I knew I was. Caitlin and Whitney bonding over shoes. I just didn't get it.

Caitlin nudged my arm. "Don't you love those shoes?"

Okay, I really didn't. My sandals were plain brown leather — like my eyes. Boring, but so comfortable.

"They don't look very comfortable," I admitted.

"What's comfort got to do with it?" Whitney asked. "It's all about style."

Which I also questioned. Jeweled shoes on a grassy knoll in a baseball park to watch fireworks?

"Hey, I thought it was the Splash team," a voice said from behind me.

I twisted my head around and looked up. It was Nick. He was holding a girl's hand. She had dark hair and a nice smile.

Sean invited them to join us, so everyone shifted around to make room for them. The girl's name was Nicole and she was Nick's girlfriend. Which meant he was now off my list of possibles.

"Nick and Nic?" Whitney asked. "Too funny."

It *was* kinda funny, but they seemed okay with it.

"Hey, we don't get to choose our names or who we like," Nick said.

"So do you work at the park?" I asked Nicole.

"No. I've got three sisters, way younger than me, so I have to babysit them during the summer while my parents are at work." She leaned against Nick. "I wish I could work there. I hear it's awesome."

"It can be," Whitney said. "Depends on your supervisor."

This from the girl who thought working at a water park meant *working* on her tan? Although maybe she was just trying to earn points with her supervisor. She smiled at Sean, he grinned back. No wonder he never got mad at her. They were in like. Disgusting.

And why was I so bothered by it?

"It also depends who else you're working with," Caitlin said, smiling at Tanner, who was grinning at her.

Who did I have to smile at? No one. It was totally unfair. Why didn't they cut the lights and start the fireworks already?

I glanced around. A guy was standing at the top of the knoll, looking right at us. I could feel his gaze. Was it possible that I might not be the only odd one out?

"Is that Jake?" I asked.

Everyone in our little group turned their head to look where I was looking. It was like I'd asked, "Is that Superman?" I almost burst out laughing, but held it back and snorted instead — which was way more embarrassing.

Sean seemed to be the only one who noticed. He grinned at me. Not exactly the way I wanted to get a guy to notice me — and Sean wasn't really a guy I was interested in. Still, I couldn't help but feel that we'd shared some sort of secret moment.

Then he shoved himself up so he was standing. He waved at Jake. Weren't we all friendly tonight?

"Who's Jake?" Caitlin asked, watching as he made his way across the grass to us.

"The ice-cream guy," Whitney said. "So is everyone from Paradise Falls here tonight?"

"A lot of them are," Caitlin said. "Makes sense, since a lot of the employees go to school here."

It didn't take Jake long to reach us. Sean made the introductions, then we played a sort of musical chairs while people shifted around trying to make more room on the quilt. Somehow Sean ended up sitting between me and Whitney. Jake sat on the other side of her. Even though I figured both Sean and Jake were interested in Whitney, it no longer looked like I didn't have anyone interested in me. Thank goodness.

But the quilt was really crowded. Still, it was nice, too. Sitting so close to a guy. I could smell the spicy soap that Sean used. When I looked at him, I could really see the blue of his eyes.

I cast a quick glance at Jake. His eyes were brown. And so not boring.

I wondered if maybe my eyes looked boring only to me. And maybe brown eyes were boring to Whitney. It was difficult to tell how she felt about Jake sitting beside her. It was pretty obvious that he liked her — why else would he have made sure to sit by her?

He still seemed kinda shy. Not talking to her or anything. Just being with her.

Maybe he was trying to figure out Sean's interest in her. She had two guys who liked her, and I had none.

The lights suddenly went out. Thank goodness. Maybe I'd stop obsessing about how hard it was to find a guy who was interested in me.

A burst of fireworks filled the black sky. The entire stadium seemed to release a collective gasp. I could see the silhouettes of everyone in our little group. Caitlin and Tanner, Nick and Nic, Jake and Whitney, Sean and —

Me?

There was just enough light to see that he was looking at me. Which made no sense since it was Whitney that he cared so much about us being nice to, Whitney he included in everything, Whitney, Whitney, Whitney . . .

Was I jealous? I thought I was. Which made no sense because he was Caitlin's brother, had always been around in my life, had irritated us both, only now I was irritated in a completely different way. Irritated that he wasn't noticing me.

Only he *was* looking at me. It was a really strange moment. An odd kind of electricity was in the air. I couldn't believe it. I was sitting there thinking about what it would be like if Sean Morgan — Caitlin's irritating brother — kissed me.

Then there was another burst of fireworks and he turned his attention back to watching the sky.

Which was a good thing. A very good thing.

CHAPTER TEN

Tuesday I was at Splash, trying not to think about Sean. I'd had this really weird dream. Sean and I were swimming, never coming up to the surface for air, like we were sea creatures or something. Every now and then a dolphin would wander by and we'd grab a fin and go zipping through the water. Laughing, laughing underwater. I'm not sure why all these images were bombarding me. It was bad enough to think about him. I didn't really want to dream about him.

"So what's up with you and Sean?" Whitney asked.

She was doing her usual thing of making sure the far side of Splash wouldn't collapse if someone sat on it. I was irritated with her for being so adorable that two guys wanted to sit by her. I was annoyed that she didn't even pretend to work.

"What do you mean?" I asked.

"You kept looking at each other last night. Do you like each other?"

"Nooo." A toddler slipped. I picked her up, helped her get situated on the slide, and gave her a little push. She laughed going down the slick slide.

"What do you think of Jake?" she asked.

"What do you mean?"

"You know, Robyn, these questions aren't that hard. They shouldn't need a translator."

"It's just that I'm distracted here trying to keep an eye on the kids. That's what we're being paid to do. Remember?"

"How can I forget when you're constantly reminding me?" She glanced around, gave one of her bored sighs.

I really couldn't figure her out. It was like she was working really hard to give the impression that everything bored her. Like last night. She'd appeared to be so excited when she arrived at the ballpark — and then she'd shifted into this-is-really-beneath-me gear. I just didn't get it. What was her story?

I heard loud, deep laughter. It wasn't unusual at a water park to hear people having fun, but near Splash, it was unusual to hear deep laughter. Deep, guy laughter.

I turned around. Three guys, grinning broadly and laughing, were swaggering toward us. They had trouble tattooed and pierced all over them. They looked way older than us, seniors in high school maybe.

The guy leading the way had a pierced eyebrow, braided leather around his neck and wrist, and a tattoo of a shark on his chest, right above his heart. I relaxed a little because I recognized the tattoo. The park had a tattoo booth near the food court. The tattoo wasn't real, just painted on, but it was waterproof — for a while anyway.

These guys had apparently stopped by the booth. For fun maybe. Or maybe they wanted to look tough.

We had four little kids at the top. I heard them screech as each one took his or her turn to go down the slide, but my attention was focused on the three guys. The attractions in Mini Falls had height restrictions. People playing here couldn't be taller than forty-eight inches.

No one else was waiting in line, which I guess made our slide a target. The guys started walking up the steps to the slide. I moved to block their way.

"Sorry, guys. This ride is for kids only."

"Whatever, loser," the lead guy said, holding up his hand, using his fingers to make a *W*, an *E*, then an *L*.

"Come on, babe, we just want to have some fun," one of the guys beside him said.

My heart was pounding. I was afraid they could hear it. "Sorry. You'll have to move on."

I heard some splashing, then Nick was standing at the side of the slide, near the top.

"Hey, guys, get out of here," Nick said.

"That's discrimination," one of the guys said. His red hair was buzzed short on the sides, but stuck up like three inches down the middle. Maybe he wanted to go down the kiddie slide because he was afraid going down a larger slide would mess up his hair. "If you don't let us go down the slide, we're gonna sue."

Why were they doing this? What was the fun in arguing? And poor Nick. It was hard for him to appear tough when he was down beside the slide. He'd have to walk around the pool to get to the steps to stand even with the guys — or he'd have to hoist himself up, which probably wouldn't look very manly.

"We're going down the slide," Shark Guy said. "So step aside."

Part of me thought, *What's the harm? Let them do it.* But rules were rules. And hadn't I, personally, gotten chewed out for not following rules? So I stood my ground, even though my stomach was starting to quiver. "No. You're not going down the slide."

I was surprised that my voice didn't shake. And where was Sean?

Suddenly a shrill whistle sounded. I jerked my head around. Whitney removed her whistle from her mouth. She was standing and grinning. "Chill, guys."

She walked up to me, so now we were a barrier of two. I felt like we were united, until she said, "Let them go down the slide."

I know my eyes did that whole widening thing —

"It's obvious they're babies," she said sweetly. "They're too chicken to do the real slides."

"Whatever, loser," Shark Guy said, doing the hand signals again.

I wondered if it was something he'd just learned, something that he thought made him cool.

"We're not afraid," one of the other guys said.

Whitney laughed. "Then why are you here? Us?" — she wiggled her finger to include me, Nick, and herself — "If we didn't have to be here, we'd be hurtling down Screaming Falls this very second. We sure wouldn't be wasting our time trying to get permission to go down a four-foot slide."

"Whatever —"

"I know. *Whatever, loser*," she said, interrupting Shark Guy and moving her hand so fast that it almost blurred. "How many times did you have to watch the video on MTV to learn that? Which you're doing wrong, by the way."

"What do you know?" Shark Guy demanded.

"I know you're about to get kicked out of the park."

"Hey, guys." It was Sean. To the rescue at last. I felt my heart slowing to a normal beat. He was waving his hand like a traffic cop telling people to come through the intersection.

Jake was standing beside him. For someone who scooped ice cream, he suddenly looked like someone you didn't want to mess with.

"Come on," Sean said. "Management wants to see you."

"Dude, we were just playing," Shark Guy said like he was three years old.

"Playing is limited to kids in this area. You know the rules. Let's go," Sean said, sounding so in charge. I wondered if his stomach was quivering like mine had been.

Sulking, the three guys headed down the steps. Sean said something to them and then made them follow him.

"You guys all right?" Jake called out.

"We're fine," I told him. At least now we were.

"What losers," Whitney said, imitating Shark Guy's hand movements.

"You handled them great," I told her.

"You weren't too bad yourself. You just forgot rule number one: Always blow your whistle when there's trouble in the area."

She actually knew the rules? Who would have thought?

"Well, I felt pretty useless," Nick said.

"Don't be silly," Whitney said. "But next time, flex those muscles."

Nick laughed. "Think I'll just blow my whistle."

"I don't understand what people are thinking when they do stuff like that," Caitlin said.

We were at lunch, sitting at a table beneath an umbrella. It's easier to talk when you can see each other. And quite honestly, lounging on the deck just made me sleepy.

Whitney and I had told her about the tough guys. I'd been as surprised by their reaction to Sean's arrival as I'd been by Whitney's confronting them. I'd pretty much figured she was useless, so now I needed to reconsider my opinion of her. Sean, well, I'd been thinking about my opinion of him way too much lately.

"They didn't give Sean a hard time at all," I told Caitlin.

"Sometimes he can look tough," she said.

Maybe he *was* tough. I remembered last night when he told us he was leaving. No room for compromise. Caitlin and I had almost tripped over ourselves to get to the car. I guess some people just have that born-to-lead gene. I thought maybe Sean was one of them.

It was weird how much I was coming to respect him. How much I was starting to like him. He made me feel good about myself, called me his go-to girl. He counted on me. And maybe I was starting to count on him.

But all these feelings were related to work. They couldn't move beyond our work environment, because the truth was that he liked Whitney. He cared about whether she was happy.

Or could it be that he cared about everyone being happy?

"Earth to Robyn. Earth to Robyn."

Fingers snapped in front of my face — and I know my eyes widened. Caitlin was snapping at me.

"What?" I asked, irritated because I wanted to examine my feelings about Sean.

"I've been trying to talk with you about tomorrow. You know? Our day off."

"Oh, right. So what did you want to do? Go shopping?"

"Actually, I'm coming here."

"You're working?"

"No, playing. Well, sorta. Mostly I want to hang around here, so Tanner can take his breaks and lunch with me. Do you want to come?"

I wouldn't mind coming to the park to play — but I'd be doing it alone.

"No, I've got some stuff I need to do."

"Like what?"

"Just stuff."

"Miss Mysterious. Okay. Whatever."

Whitney and I were walking back to Splash when she said, "You don't really have stuff to do tomorrow, do you?"

"So what gave me away? My eyes turned purple?"

"What?" she asked.

"Nothing. But yes, you're right. I don't have anything to do tomorrow. I just didn't want to be a third wheel — again."

Which meant I'd be a lone wheel. I wasn't sure I wanted to be that either, but what choice did I have?

CHAPTER ELEVEN

The next morning I rolled out of bed without a purpose. I didn't have to go to work. Mom had taken care of the dust bunnies a few days ago so I was pretty sure none had multiplied since then — and if they had, well, I wasn't going to go looking for them.

So I had the whole day to myself and I wasn't quite sure what to do with it. I almost always hung out with Caitlin. Usually at the mall, sometimes at a movie, occasionally in her bedroom scouring through all her teen mags for the answers to life's toughest questions. Like how to give yourself a professional-looking pedicure in ten minutes or how to lessen the sting when plucking your eyebrows. Not that I was plucking my eyebrows yet, but when I was ready, I'd be prepared.

So I stumbled around my room getting dressed. I was sure Mom had already left for work. When I was dressed, with my hair clipped in back, I walked to the window and just looked outside. Caitlin's house was two streets over. Since my bedroom was on the second floor, I had no problem seeing the roof of her house.

What really bothered me was that I was wondering what Sean was doing today. He wasn't working either. I guess he was going to take Caitlin to the water park and then either hang around there or go home. I wondered if I'd gone if he would have hung around with me. Probably not. But I was a little interested in knowing what might have happened if Whitney wasn't around.

He and I had been getting along fine at the ballpark, talking and everything until Whitney showed up. If she hadn't shown up would he have still sat on the quilt with us? Would it have been like he was there with me?

I was still looking out the window when a car caught my eye. A white car. No, not a car. A limo. What was a limo doing on our street?

It came to a stop in front of our house and my heart nearly stopped. What if it was Stacy and Clinton from *What Not to Wear*? What if Mom and I were going to get a clothing makeover? Or maybe it was someone coming to make over the house?

A front door opened and a man — dressed like a chauffeur in a movie — got out and walked around to a back door. He opened it —

All the while I was holding my breath. I had a feeling our lives were about to change —

And then Whitney stepped out.

Whitney? In a limo?

She walked toward the door. I was too stunned to move. The doorbell rang. This was just too much.

It rang again.

She was probably expecting my butler to answer the door.

I hurried down the stairs, then wondered why I was rushing for her. What was it about her that made people respond like she was a princess or something? I slowed my step, then my curiosity spiraled and I found myself hurrying once again. I opened the door.

"Hey," Whitney said brightly.

"You drive around in a limo?"

She laughed, like she was embarrassed. "What? Oh, yeah, that. My dad had to work today so he rented a limo for me. It's no big deal. He's feeling guilty. Do you want to ride around in it?"

"Uh . . ." Did I? Maybe. "I don't know. How'd you know where I live?"

"I asked Mr. T."

"And he just gave you my information?"

"Well, uh, yeah. See, helping with those parties over the weekend just really put me in a party mood, and I thought it would be great fun to have an employee get-together after work Sunday night. And I told him you'd help me plan it, so" — she lifted her shoulders — "will you?"

"You volunteered me without asking me?" Did she think everyone did what she wanted? I wasn't Sean, who was wrapped around her finger.

"I thought you'd want to. Why wouldn't you?"

She seemed completely baffled.

"Shouldn't you have asked me first, though?"

"Well, I would have if I'd known it was such a big deal. I just figured you'd want to help with a party. Who doesn't want to help? But if you don't, I can tell Mr. T you weren't interested. I can do it by myself."

It was a little sad that she'd come to me. We weren't really friends. Did she even have any friends?

"I might be interested. I have to think about it. Do you want to come in?"

"That'd be great. Thanks." Whitney looked back over her shoulder and waved.

"Just letting David know that I'm coming in."

"Who's David?" I asked.

"The chauffeur. He has to stay with the car."

Whitney walked inside and looked around. I didn't want to look at my house through her eyes. It was mostly decorated with stuff from Target, but Mom always pronounced it Tarjay — like it was French and fancy. I wasn't totally convinced that all Whitney's stuff were really knockoffs. And now that she'd arrived in a limo —

My stomach rumbled. I felt the embarrassment warm my cheeks. "I haven't had breakfast yet. I was going to make a peanut butter sandwich."

"For breakfast?"

"My culinary skills are limited. Do you want a sandwich?"

"No thanks, but you go ahead. I've never seen one being made."

"You're kidding?"

"No, we eat out a lot. It's just my dad and

me since Mom died, and Mom never cooked either, so . . ."

While she rambled, I led her back to the kitchen.

"Nice house," Whitney said.

Was she actually giving compliments? This was really a little weird.

When we got to the kitchen, she sat at the counter and I grabbed all the sandwich makings. "So what does your dad do?"

"Oh, you know. He's involved in some business. Boring stuff. I don't pay much attention."

After I finished making my sandwich, I offered Whitney something to drink, but she wasn't interested. I poured myself some milk and sat at the counter. "I just realized that I don't even know where you go to school."

"It's a private school. Very private. You've probably never heard of it. So are your parents around?"

"It's just me and Mom. Dad left when I was little. I don't even know him."

"Oh, gosh, sorry. What a jerk! My dad's okay. Just overprotective."

"Mom's pretty neat. She's at work right now, though."

I couldn't believe that Whitney and I were actually talking like normal people. She was revealing things about herself. Not in great detail, but I was getting a glimpse into her life.

"So will you help me plan the party?" she asked.

"You want to plan a party for all the employees?"

"Well, duh, yeah. I don't want anyone feeling left out."

"Do you have any idea how many employees there are?"

"Two hundred and forty-five."

"You know the exact number?"

She looked guilty about something, like she was trying to think of the answer. "Well, yeah. I mean, I asked Mr. T."

"Where could you have a party for that many people?"

"At the water park. After it closes." She leaned forward. "Look, all we have to do is come up with a list of things that we want to happen. I'll give the list to Mr. T. His staff will take care of it. It's not like we have to actually *do* anything."

Again, it seemed odd that she'd come to me.

"Anything we want?" I asked.

"Look, it's like my dad always says, you always reach as far as you can. If you don't make it, you're still farther along than you would have been if you didn't reach at all. Corny, I know, but his point is, we ask for everything we want. We might not get it. We probably won't get it. But even if we don't, we still have something. So are you in or not?"

I couldn't think of a reason not to be.

"I'm in!"

We spent an hour at the counter tossing ideas back and forth. Whitney knew a lot — I mean, a *lot* — about the park and how it operated. She knew the things we could use without too much hassle — like all the water stuff that just needed lifeguards, not attendants. There wouldn't be lifeguards on duty, but since we were all essentially lifeguards, we didn't need any on duty. We didn't want anyone having to work. And food. The dishes that were easy to prepare. Things that could just be set up — like the ice-cream and drink carts — that we could just take things from. I was amazed by her knowledge. I'd been going to the park as a guest for a few years and there were things I hadn't noticed.

"It just seems boring," she said.

"How can it be boring?" I asked. "We'll have a chance to play, to go down slides without getting yelled at."

"Still I want something different. Something . . . I don't know. Exciting. Something that's never been done at the park before."

"Like what?"

"If I knew, then I'd know."

She wasn't much help. But then maybe she didn't think I was either. She was scribbling on a pad of paper, then she stopped, looked at me. "My dad goes driving when he has a problem he needs to figure out. So, you want to take a drive in the limo?"

Okay, it might be geeky but I really did want to ride around in the limo.

"I'd love to."

I called Mom at work and told her what was going on. She was okay with it.

The inside of the limo was spacious, luxurious. Lots of leg room. The seats were leather. The windows were tinted. We could see out, but no one could see in. Whitney reached into a little fridge and handed me a soda.

This definitely wasn't a knockoff.

She told the driver to start driving until she figured out where she wanted to go. It was such a smooth ride.

"Wow," I said, totally amazed. "This is really awesome."

"A sports car would be more fun. Anyway, what can we do that's different?"

I took a sip of the cola. Shook my head. "I don't know."

"Money's no object."

I laughed. "You think the park owners are going to want to spend a lot of money on this?"

"I just mean that we can think big, not worry about cost, and the owners can say no. Or not. Who knows? They might surprise us."

"I can't think of anything different. When I'm at the park, I like to play in the water. And we'll be doing that."

"True. But think big, different. Bold."

I looked out the window. We passed a movie theater. Maybe when Whitney got tired of playing party planner, I'd go to a movie. Alone. Gag. Then something started teasing me.

"Okay," I said. "I might have an idea."

"Spill it."

"Well, it's kinda out there."

"Robyn — reach!"

"Okay. Okay." I was used to Caitlin being the one with the ideas, the one who said what we did, when we did it. This was a little scary, which was silly really. The worst she could do was laugh.

"What if we showed a movie?"

"I don't get it," Whitney said. "Like in the little theater they use for talent shows every now and then? What's special about that?"

"No, not indoors. Outdoors. Like when they used to have drive-in theaters. But this would be a *float*-in theater."

"I still don't get it."

I was doing a lousy job of explaining.

"Well, you know that big white wall behind Tsunami?"

"Yeah."

"We could set up a projector on the roof of the pavilion across from it and show a movie on that wall. Have people in inner tubes in the pool area, not run the waves of course, or maybe we would — I don't know.

But we could do a movie like *Jaws* or *Open Water* — kinda like, not only watch it but experience it."

Whitney smiled. "That's not a bad idea. As a matter of fact, it could be genius. I mean, if it works for the employees, then maybe we could have a movie night for guests — something special. I like it. I'll talk to my dad about it," Whitney said.

"Why would your dad care?" I asked.

"Oh, he wouldn't, but he does a lot of business stuff, so maybe he'll have an idea about it, can tell me how to pitch it so the TPTB are convinced."

"You really think they'll go for it?"

"Most definitely," Whitney said. "Trust me. I always get what I want."

CHAPTER TWELVE

The next morning on the ride into work, I told Sean and Caitlin all about the party. I was pretty pumped, talking like I'd had way too much caffeine. Whitney had called me last night to let me know that the party had been approved and that they were even looking into my movie idea.

"Can you believe it?" I asked. "Whitney says that if the float-in movie works for the party, they might even do it as a special night at the park for guests."

"Do you know how many times you've mentioned her name since you got in the car?" Caitlin asked.

"Well, she's part of this. I mean, we planned this together."

"Didn't I tell you that you'd like Whitney?" Sean said, grinning.

"I don't know if I'd go that far. Well, maybe I would. She seemed so different yesterday. Well, except for the whole limo experience."

"I can't believe you went driving around in a limo and didn't call me," Caitlin said.

"You were busy."

"Still."

When we got to the water park, Caitlin and I hung back while Sean hurried to get to work. He had another supervisors' meeting, which worked for Caitlin and me because it gave us a chance to talk.

"So how were things with Tanner yesterday?" I asked.

"Awesome." She grinned broadly. "He gave me a ride home."

"Did he kiss you?"

"No, but I think he wants to. Or at least I want him to. I found out he plays on his high school football team so he can only work through July — then he'll have to start practice."

"So that's the reason he looks so strong."

"Yeah," she said, bobbing her head. "Because he's really a jock. Pretty cool, huh?"

"Very cool."

When we got to the employee locker rooms, we discovered flyers announcing EMPLOYEE GET ACQUAINTED NIGHT taped to every locker.

"Wow! Whitney works fast," Caitlin said, taking the flyer off her locker. "I really hope this gives me a chance to hang out with Tanner when he's not working."

Caitlin and I had always hung out at the water park together. I couldn't imagine going through the park, rushing down the slides, experiencing all the thrills and spills that the park had to offer without her. But I guess it was only fair — things between us were changing a little. Me missing lunch. Me hanging out with Whitney.

"So you and Tanner — you like each other that much already? I mean, to hang out together, for the whole night?"

"Yeah. I think so. Or at least that's what I'm planning on."

Which meant I had to find a guy to hang out with — and quick.

"Okay, we need to stop by the mall on the way home," Caitlin said after we got in the car. It was Saturday evening after work and the big bash was tomorrow. "Employee Get Acquainted Night — I need a new bathing suit."

"I thought you just bought one," Sean said.

"I did, but I need another one."

"Caitlin —"

"Come on, Sean. It'll be almost eight thirty when we get there, so I'll be forced to shop fast. It's thirty minutes out of your life."

He grumbled some more, before agreeing to take us to the mall. As we drove, I wondered where Caitlin got the energy to go shopping. I was exhausted. Maybe it was more tiring watching little kids all day instead of cute guys. And in typical Caitlin fashion, she'd figured if she needed to shop for a bathing suit, I did, too.

For most of lunch, Whitney and I had listened to Caitlin talking about how much she liked Tanner, every cute thing that he did, and how she planned to spend time with him during the employee bash. I was glad he was showing interest in her. Really, I was. But how many different ways could you say a guy was cute?

The good thing, if there was a good thing, was that Caitlin and Whitney weren't being catty toward each other anymore. I couldn't tell if they really liked each other yet, but at least they weren't putting each other down.

When we got to the mall, Sean parked near the main entrance. As we walked inside, Sean said, "Call me when you're ready. I'll be at the food court."

"Oh, that sounds so good," I said, without thinking.

Caitlin looked at me like I'd just told her the mall had disappeared. She's a shop-till-she-drops kind of girl. Usually I am, too, but tonight I was tired, hungry, and didn't need a bathing suit.

"What about the employee party?" she asked.

"I've got something to wear."

She pulled me aside. "That night is our chance —"

"I know, but I'm tired *and* hungry."

"Fine. I'll meet y'all at the food court."

She headed off and I felt the need to yell an apology after her. Then I realized it was just Sean and me. I had an urge to run after her then. I'd responded from survival instincts — wanting to eat. And now —

Sean was looking at me like it had just dawned on him that I was joining him at the food court and he didn't know what to do with me.

"We should probably get up there before they start shutting down," he said.

"Yeah."

Okay, it was just Sean, Caitlin's brother. It wasn't like he was on my "Top Ten Guys" list.

Although he certainly could be. Quite honestly, I was a little confused about how I was feeling about him these days. I was thinking about him way too much.

We took the escalators to the second floor and the food court. We parted ways. He went to the left, I went to the right. We both ended up standing in line for quick Chinese. After we got our food — he went with a noodle bowl, I went with fried rice — we sat at a table at the edge of the food court.

"I like to people-watch," he said.

"Usually I like to shop," I said, which I guess made me one of the people he might have watched. "But I'm so tired."

"Caitlin has some sort of crazy shopping gene," he said.

I tried not to stare at him; it was really weird sitting here with him and almost talking like two people who liked each other.

"So, really, how do you like working at the park?" he asked.

"Really?"

He grinned, nodded, before using chopsticks to gather up his noodles. I'd never mastered the use of chopsticks, which made me feel self-conscious as I used my fork.

"It's not nearly as exciting as I thought it would be. I'm really just standing around watching people."

"It's definitely more fun to be a guest."

"How do you like being a supervisor?"

"It's harder than I thought — especially when I have to get after someone for misbehaving. I never realized how many people goof off."

"People like Whitney?"

"She's doing better."

He was always defending her. "Do you like her?" I asked.

"Well, yeah, don't you?"

Guys can be so dense. "I meant, like, you know. Girlfriend, like."

He laughed. "What is it with you and Caitlin? Always trying to figure out who I like."

"*Is* there someone you like?" I asked.

He poked his noodles. "Yeah, there is."

I didn't know why I was disappointed to hear that.

"Do I know her?"

He looked up, held my gaze. "Yeah, I think you do."

"Are you going to tell me who?" I asked.

"I don't think so. At least not yet. So, is there someone you like?" he asked.

Okay, this was weird. It was like a question Caitlin would ask, something I'd tell her. Not something I'd tell her older brother, who also happened to be my supervisor.

"I like a lot of people," I said.

"Not fair. I confessed."

"You didn't confess. You hinted."

He went back to eating his noodles. I went back to eating my rice.

What had we been doing? Talking, sure, but it seemed like there was more to it. Maybe a little *what*? Flirting?

No, we were just killing time.

"Hey, guys," Caitlin said, dropping down in a chair between us.

Sean and I both jumped, like maybe we'd been doing something we weren't supposed to.

"I found the cutest red bikini," Caitlin said.

"You've got a red bathing suit," Sean said.

"That's my uniform. It doesn't count. You just so don't get it."

He'd finished off his noodles, and I was stuffed. They announced that the mall would be closing in five minutes.

"Guess we'd better go," Sean said.

We tossed our trash. He was walking

ahead of us as we went toward the exit. Caitlin opened her bag.

"Look, isn't it the cutest?"

I know she was talking about the bathing suit, like I could really see what it looked like, folded up at the bottom of the bag.

But when I said, "Yes, totally cute," I didn't think I was talking about the bikini. I thought maybe I was talking about her brother.

CHAPTER THIRTEEN

What kind of party had rules?

Ours did.

Any ride that required someone actually work it — like Screaming Falls — was closed. Since no lifeguards were officially on duty — but lifeguards were everywhere — we had access to all other areas of the park. We were supposed to watch out for each other, always do things in pairs. No one, according to Mr. T when he made the announcement, was supposed to be a lone wolf.

The kiosks with drinks and ice cream and snacks were left full and unattended. We could just take what we wanted.

For the first hour, Mr. T and the manager of each section were at Scavenger's cooking up free hot dogs for anyone who wanted them.

"This is really cool," I said to Whitney when we sat at a table with our dogs. "Did you have any idea that they'd do all this for us?"

She shrugged and took a bite. "I'd hoped."

"It must be costing them a fortune."

"Not really. Hot dogs are cheap. So what if all the employees have a couple of them? It's not that much. We'll have happy employees and happy employees work harder."

She sounded like some sort of commercial.

"Including you?"

She laughed. "Not me. This was just an excuse for a party." She nodded her head to the side. "So, it looks like Caitlin got her guy."

I looked over my shoulder. Caitlin was

sitting at a table with Tanner. She was smiling, looking happy.

"Yeah, I think she did." I wondered if he'd kiss her tonight.

"Hey."

I jerked around at the familiar voice. Sean sat between Whitney and me.

"This is pretty cool," he said before taking a bite of a hot dog. He was wearing black swim trunks, a black tank top, and black flip-flops.

"You're really into black, aren't you?" I said.

"You know it. Wearing the park uniform . . . it's torture to put it on every day."

"Guys, I'm going to go get us all an ice cream," Whitney said.

It looked like Sean was going to object, maybe offer to go with her, but she'd headed out before she'd finished telling us what she planned to do. Which left me alone with Sean. It wasn't that I really felt uncomfortable being with him. I was just having a difficult time understanding our relationship.

Quite honestly, I was spending more time talking to him lately than I was spending with Caitlin.

Sean finished off his hot dog. I tried to make an origami swan with my limp napkin — which really didn't work too well.

"So . . . have you been on the Bermuda Triangle this year?" he asked.

"All work and no play —"

"Makes us both dull, right?"

I smiled. "I'm not dull." Or maybe I was, I thought, as I looked at my limp swan.

"Hey, guys," Whitney said, coming back over without ice cream. "We're going to do a train at the Bermuda Triangle. Come on, let's go."

She had about a dozen people with her. Nick and Jake and a couple of other guys and some girls I hadn't met.

Before I could even decide if this was something I wanted to do, Sean grabbed my hand. "All work and no play — we're the two dullest people here."

"Speak for yourself," I said, laughing.

183

"Caitlin, Tanner! Come on," Whitney called out. "We're going to break the Guinness World Record with a train of people going down a slide."

"Is that even a record that's recorded?" Sean asked me.

"I don't know."

He was still holding my hand, but I figured it was just, I don't know, reflex maybe. I was sure it didn't mean anything — to him at least.

It was kind of a strange thing to realize that it actually meant something to me. I wondered when I started to like him — as more than Caitlin's brother, as more than my supervisor. The truth was I didn't want anyone else holding my hand. I didn't want to go down the slide with anyone else.

But there were so many people that I realized I probably could end up with someone else — unless Sean didn't let go of my hand. So I did something that I, shy Robyn, never did. I held on so he couldn't let go.

When we got to the Bermuda Triangle, everyone gathered around the stairs that would take us to the top of the slide. Gathered because Whitney was blocking the entrance.

"Okay, everyone listen. We have to go up boy girl boy girl. At the top, we all sit down, put our arms around the person in front of us, then the train will start going down the slide — don't let go."

"Is this safe?" someone asked.

"Probably not. But who cares? Chickens stay behind. The rest of you, let's go."

"As a supervisor, I probably shouldn't do this," Sean said as people edged past us.

"You're not a supervisor right now," I said. "At this moment, you're just an employee."

"I guess. Okay, I'll do it. Let's go."

When we got to the top, we were the last in line. I put my arms around Tanner who had his arms around Caitlin. Sean put his arms around me and I almost stopped breathing. I liked it so much. I liked him holding me.

"Everyone ready!" Whitney yelled.

A resounding chorus of "*Yes!*" echoed around us.

"Let's do it," she shouted.

We heard screams as people started going down the slide. Of course, we hadn't given any thought to the logistics of moving forward to the edge of the slide while still sitting.

"Ah!" Caitlin yelled. "The chain broke."

"That's okay," Tanner said. "Two's more fun anyway."

I let go of him, and he and Caitlin moved to the edge of the slide and went over together.

"Guess it's just us," Sean said.

I looked back at him. "I guess so."

"So, do you want to do it solo?"

I shook my head. "Not really."

"Okay."

We moved to the top of the slide and sat down. He put his arms around me. "Ready," he asked near my ear.

A shiver went down my spine. I nodded.

"Here we go!"

He shoved off, pushing himself and me over the edge. We were hurtling down the slide —

And suddenly there was no slide. Just the emptiness. I don't know how he held on to me, but he did and we plunged into the water together. Sean was heavier, he was going deeper so he let go of me.

When I broke through to the surface, I was sputtering and laughing. Sean popped up just a few seconds later.

"That was fun," he said. "Maybe I've spent too much of my life trying to do the right thing."

It seemed like a confession of sorts. I didn't totally understand why, but it made me feel like he was talking about something else. Suddenly I was very much aware of him as a guy — not as Caitlin's brother.

"Race you to the edge of the pool," I said.

I swam as hard as I could, trying not to think about all these crazy feelings and thoughts that were jumbling around inside me. But no matter how hard I swam, I was no match for Sean. He reached the edge of the pool first and hefted himself out of the water. Then he reached down to give me a hand up.

I put my hand in his and wondered when he'd gotten so strong. When he pulled me out of the water, and I was standing in front of him breathing heavily, I wondered when being close to him started making my heart thump.

"So what's next?" he asked.

"The rapids?"

"Let's go."

He took my hand again, and it made me wonder what he'd say if I told him the truth — that what I really wanted next was a kiss.

It was kinda strange. Sean and I ended up doing all of the rides together. Whitney had disappeared to who-knows-where, with who-knows-who, and Caitlin was hanging out with Tanner.

The first time our paths crossed after the Bermuda Triangle, Caitlin had given me a big grin, like she was absolutely happy, totally into Tanner. The next time, maybe some of the novelty had worn off, because she'd given me a what-are-you-still-doing-with-my-brother look.

But she wasn't so worried about it that she was going to leave Tanner to find out what was going on. I was glad because I wasn't really sure what was going on. I was having fun with Sean.

"Do you like Screaming Falls?" he asked.

"It's my favorite. I was really sorry they closed it down for the night."

"You can keep a secret, right?"

"Oh, yeah. No problem."

"You can't even tell Caitlin — and you absolutely can't tell Whitney, because we'd all get in trouble."

"I know the party was Whitney's idea, but it's not like she's the boss. And she's not exactly Miss-do-everything-she's-supposed-to-do either."

"Still, she . . . we just don't want her to know about this."

"Who is 'we' and what is 'this'?"

"I'm putting my job in your hands."

Then he put my hand in his and started pulling me off toward the shadows. They hadn't left any lights on in this area, because we weren't supposed to do the rides in this section of Thrill Hill. Most required an attendant.

Sean turned a corner and started leading me up the stairs that would take us to the top of Screaming Falls.

"Wait, what are we doing?" I asked.

"I can't tell you because I swore I wouldn't tell a nonsupervisor —"

I heard a scream and then a splash.

"Are y'all doing the slide?"

He put his finger to my mouth. "*Shh.* We gotta hurry before we get caught."

I laughed. "You're not Mister-I-never-do-anything-I'm-not-supposed-to-do."

"Keep it a secret, okay?" he said as he pulled me up the steps.

Lisa was waiting at the top. "Morgan, supervisors only."

"She won't tell."

He pulled me into the booth and closed the door.

"We're going to do —"

The floor dropped out before I could finish asking him if we were doing this together. I hadn't even realized that he'd wrapped his arms around me and I'd wrapped mine around him. But we were hurtling down another slide, holding each other.

It was fun and exhilarating.

I liked this slightly bad Sean — the one who wanted to have a good time. We hit the water, went under, bounced back up. Then we were swimming to the side to get out as quickly as possible — before we were discovered.

They sounded the alarm to signal that they were going to start turning off the water to the various slides.

Sean and I started walking toward Tsunami where we'd left our stuff on lounge chairs earlier. We'd been so comfortable going down slides together, traveling through the rapids. Now suddenly we were quiet, almost like strangers.

I wanted to say something, but I couldn't think of anything clever — or at least un-stupid — sounding.

Caitlin was waiting for us at the lounging deck. "Tanner is going to take me home," she announced. "I already called Mom and she said it was okay."

But she hadn't asked me if it was okay. She was leaving me to ride home alone with her brother. What was wrong with her?

I guess when it came to choosing between a possible boyfriend or a best friend that she was going to choose the possible boyfriend.

"All right," Sean said.

"I'll talk to you later," Caitlin said.

Maybe she was getting back at me for hanging out with Whitney. But that just wasn't Caitlin. We were on the same team always. Unfortunately we'd had so much going on that we really hadn't had a chance to talk, and she had no idea that I was starting to have all these thoughts about her brother. But even if we did have time, I couldn't tell her that I was starting to like Sean. She'd never understand.

She thought he was irritating.

I watched her and Tanner walk off, holding hands.

"Seems kinda serious," I said to no one in particular.

"Yeah," Sean said, reminding me that he was standing nearby.

"I wonder if Whitney could give me a ride home," I murmured.

"What?"

I looked over at him. "Well, I just hate for you to have to go to the trouble —"

"We live in the same neighborhood."

"I know, but I know you put up with me because I'm Caitlin's friend."

He stared at me for a minute, shook his head, and sighed. Then he shifted his gaze past me. "Whitney, can you give Robyn a ride home?"

"What? Oh, sure."

"Sean —"

"It's okay. I get it. You're Caitlin's friend. I'll pick you up in the morning."

Watching him walk away, I wondered what had just happened.

I heard Whitney's flip-flops slapping the ground as she walked over. She had a towel wrapped around her waist, her wet hair caught up in back with a jeweled clip.

"What was all that about?" she asked.

"I don't know."

"I saw you guys hanging out. I thought maybe . . ." Her voice trailed off.

"Maybe what?"

"That you liked each other. You're always hanging out together."

"I thought he liked you. I mean, he never yells at you for not working and he always wants to make sure you're happy."

"What are you talking about?"

"He's always looking out for you, telling me to be friends with you —"

"So you're friends with me because he told you to be?"

My night was going from bad to worse. "In the beginning, yes, but not so much now. I mean, now I like you. I want to be friends."

"Well, geez, thanks so much."

She started walking toward the entrance.

I glanced around. Almost everyone had left.

"Are you still giving me a ride?" I called out after her, grabbing my tote bag, and hurrying to catch up with her.

"Don't see that I have much choice. Who else are you going to ride home with?"

Mr. T was standing at the entrance, adding a personal touch, saying good night to the employees.

"Great idea, Whitney," he said as she and I walked through. "Went over really well. Sorry we couldn't get the movie set up here in time, but it's in the works and as soon as it's ready we'll have employee movie night."

"Thanks, Mr. T."

"Good night, Robyn," he said.

I nearly tripped over my feet. He knew who I was? "'Night."

The white stretch limo was waiting near the front.

"Your dad had to work again?" I asked.

"Yep."

The driver opened the door for us.

"David, we're taking Robyn home."

"Yes, Miss Whitney."

He had a wonderful British accent that reminded me of James Bond.

Whitney and I crawled inside. I settled back against the seat. "So your dad works a lot."

"Oh, yeah. All the time. But that is so boring to talk about. So do you like Sean or not?"

I groaned, wishing I could just disappear into the seat. "Yes. Do you?"

"I like him, but I don't want him for a boyfriend."

"But he might want you for a girlfriend," I told her.

"If that was true, why was he holding your hand tonight?"

"Because yours wasn't around?"

She laughed. "Are you really that dense? Do you not see the way he looks at you?"

"I guess not."

"He likes you. Big-time. So are you going to tell Caitlin you like him?"

"No!" I buried my face in my hands. "She so won't understand." I peered through my fingers at Whitney. "Caitlin thinks he's irritating."

"Of course she does. He's her brother. What's important is what you think."

Was I actually considering confessing everything to Adorable Girl?

"I thought he was irritating, too, until this summer. And now, I . . . I don't know. I like him. He works hard, and he's nice, and he worries about people. And he's fun."

And he knew so much about me, like

maybe he'd been noticing things about me all along — while I'd only started noticing things about him this summer. Was it possible that he'd never talked to me before because he liked me and didn't know how to tell me? That maybe he worried about what Caitlin would think as much as I did?

I always thought that the first time I started falling for someone that I'd talk to Caitlin about him. But I couldn't tell Caitlin. And here was Whitney willing to listen. When had I become friends enough with Whitney to tell her how I was feeling?

Everything was changing this summer. I was so confused.

"So what you are going to do?" Whitney asked.

"I don't know. What if tonight was just an aberration? What if we were hanging out together because there was no one else?"

"There were plenty of other people. I think he was with you because he wanted to be. The real question is: Why were you with him?"

CHAPTER FOURTEEN

When Whitney dropped me off at home, she offered to give me a ride to work the next day, which meant that I needed to let Sean know not to pick me up. But I didn't have his cell number, which was a good thing / bad thing. Good because I didn't have to talk to him. Bad because I had to talk to Caitlin.

I was sitting on my bed, staring at my cell phone trying to figure out how to say what I needed to say. When had I started to worry about telling Caitlin anything? We'd been friends forever. We always confided in each other. She never judged me.

Maybe I'd just never done anything that needed judging.

I was about to quick-dial Caitlin when my phone rang. It was her.

"Hey," I said when I answered.

"What were you doing hanging out with my brother?"

Just like Caitlin to get straight to the point.

"How was your date with Tanner?" I asked, trying for a subject change. "Did he kiss you?"

"No, he didn't." She sounded majorly disappointed. I didn't blame her. He was cute and they'd hung out all night.

"But you were together all night."

"And you were with my brother. Did he kiss you?"

"No."

"Did you want him to?"

"Caitlin, let's talk about you and Tanner."

"You did!"

"Caitlin, *shh*! He listens at the door."

"What? No, he doesn't."

"Sometimes he does. Listen, I want to talk about you and Tanner."

"I need to know what's going on with you and my brother. He's acting weird. I can't explain it. It's like he's upset, and I don't like to see him upset. What did you say to him?"

"Nothing. Things have suddenly gotten really complicated. Whitney is giving me a ride to work in the morning."

"Whitney? What is it with you and Whitney? Is she your new best friend?"

"She's my new friend. You're my best friend. You'll always be my best friend. But just tell Sean not to come get me on his way to work tomorrow morning."

"I don't even know who you are anymore."

Would it make her feel better if I said that I didn't know either?

"I'll see you at lunch," I told her. Then I hung up before she could say anything else.

I rolled over onto my side, curled up, and tried to make sense of things. But no matter how hard I thought about everything, nothing made sense.

It was a little pretentious arriving at Paradise Falls in a limo.

"Does your dad always work?" I asked Whitney as we were walking to the employee entrance.

"Pretty much."

"Is the limo really rented?"

"No, it's just a little embarrassing to be driven around. I really can't wait until I'm sixteen. Although I'm not getting a *used* car."

I smiled at that. "Must be nice."

"Yeah, maybe I'll get that knockoff Ferrari that Caitlin was talking about."

I was really starting to like Whitney. I thought she came from a different world than I did and that maybe Mom had been right: Her dad wanted her to work so she'd learn the value of money. But our friendship wasn't to the point where I could really ask her something that personal.

"So who were you hanging out with last night?" I asked her instead.

"Lots of different people. I like partying. I don't like settling on one person."

I pushed open the door that led into the employee locker room. "But you want a boyfriend, don't you?"

"Maybe. Yeah. Sure. Someday. When the right guy comes along."

When we got to our lockers, I saw Caitlin standing there — like maybe she'd been waiting for me.

"You're almost late," she said.

"Almost doesn't count."

I opened my locker, tossed my tote inside, and took off my shorts and T-shirt. My bathing suit was on underneath.

"So, will I see you at lunch?" she asked.

"Yeah, definitely."

"Okay."

She headed out, but I thought maybe she had something else she wanted to say. And I had a lot that I needed to say to her.

"I'll catch you later," I said to Whitney, then I rushed out of the locker room. "Caitlin, wait!"

She stopped walking and I hurried over.

"I like Whitney," I said. "She's my friend."

"That's cool. You always wanted us to be a bigger group."

"Maybe sometime the three of us can do something together — away from the park. She gets driven around in a limo."

"You're kidding?"

"Nope. And all her knockoffs? I don't think they're really knockoffs."

"So why is she working here?"

"I don't know."

"Mmm. Well, maybe we both need to start paying more attention to her. I'll see you at lunch."

I watched her walk away. Maybe I'd worked out the friendship part of my life. Now if I could just figure out the rest of it.

I couldn't believe it. Even though I'd taken time to talk to Caitlin, I still got to Splash before Whitney did.

Nick was already there. "Thought I was going to be working solo," he said.

"I think you could handle it," I said.

"Yeah, me too. Really, I think they need to move us around."

"You don't have to convince me."

Although now I liked working here, because it meant that I saw Sean a little more. Or at least usually I did.

He wasn't around either, which made me wonder if he and Whitney were off doing something together.

Did she like him? Would she tell me if she did? She'd told me the limo was rented, indicated it was a one-time thing but it wasn't. What else had she told me that wasn't true?

I finally spotted her practically skipping toward us. Obviously happy. Maybe they'd given her a job somewhere else.

Only I wasn't sure that I wanted her working somewhere else. Yes, she was a little quirky and not completely into actually working, but she was getting better at it.

"They figured out how to do the movie setup that we wanted. The equipment should arrive in the next couple of days," she said when she got to Splash. "It's gonna be awesome. We're going to have another party and if it works the way that I think it will, we'll start having one late night a week with a movie — for the guests."

"That would mean we'd have to work extra," I pointed out.

"Overtime pay." She wiggled her eyebrows. "That would be cool, huh?"

"I didn't think you wanted to work at all."

"It's growing on me. Of course, we'd have to have family films," she said, like she was creating the schedule in her head. "Like *Finding Nemo* or *The Little Mermaid*. We need to come up with a list of appropriate water films. For us — the employees — it's going to be *Jaws*."

I gave a little shudder. "Just the thought of it gives me chills."

And I could imagine guys going underwater and trying to scare us. I grinned. Might be fun.

"So what did you decide about Sean?" Whitney asked after a moment.

We were standing there, holding our rescue tubes, just watching kids slide, every now and then telling them to settle down. Like they listened to us.

"Nothing. I haven't even seen him today."

"He was in the office waiting to talk to Mr. T when I was in there."

"About what?"

She shrugged. "He didn't say. I mean, why would he tell me?"

"I don't know. Y'all seem kinda close. That first day you were having lunch together."

"He's just looking out for me, because they asked him to."

"Who asked him to?"

She waved her hand like it was nothing. "It's not important."

"You know, sometimes you make me feel like . . . I don't know. Like, maybe you have secrets."

"We all have secrets. You know that little boy out there sure can hold his breath for a long time."

"What little boy?"

"The one floating in the Lost Lagoon."

I spun around and saw him. He was maybe three or four. Where was his mother?

"Nick, call for help!" I yelled. Nick ran down toward the office as I jumped over the edge of Splash and landed in the Lost Lagoon. I started wading, trudging, toward the little boy.

I heard another splash. It was Whitney coming up beside me.

"Isn't he playing?" Whitney asked.

"I don't think so."

I got to him, turned him over. His lips were blue. I lifted him up and hurried back to Splash where we'd at least have an area with only maybe a quarter of an inch or so of water, which kept the cement from getting hot. People used it as a path.

I set the little boy down on the cool cement and climbed up out of the lagoon. Whitney was right beside me.

"What do I do?" she asked. "I don't know what to do."

I didn't have time to explain. I started breathing into the little boy's mouth, remembering everything they'd taught us in CPR class, tilting his chin back. Two quick breaths, then pumping on his chest. Counting the pumps. Then two more quick breaths.

The little boy coughed, spit up some water, and started crying.

It was the first time I was ever glad to hear a kid cry.

"There!" I heard someone shout.

I looked over and a woman was rushing over with a couple of other people, Nick, an EMT, and Sean. The EMT got there first and started checking the boy's vitals. I heard Whitney telling the woman she was going to have to wait.

Sean pulled me to my feet.

"Are you okay?" he asked.

"Yeah." Only then did I realize that I was trembling. "You're all blurry."

"That's 'cause you're crying. It's okay." He put his arms around me and held me. It felt really good. Suddenly I was cold and he was warm. "You're a hero."

"Whitney helped," I said. "And Nick."

"I didn't do anything," Whitney said.

"Come on. We need to get you warm," Sean said.

I looked back at the medic. "Is he going to be okay?"

"Looks like." He winked at me. "You did a good job."

"Thanks. But if Whitney hadn't seen him —"

"Will you shut up already?" she asked. "You did it by yourself."

"No, I didn't. We're a team."

"You can argue about it later," Sean said.

He took me to the first aid station and wrapped a warm blanket around me, like I was in shock or something.

"See, I knew you were dependable," he said quietly.

"Why do you make all these exceptions for Whitney?" I asked. Maybe I *was* in shock because the question seemed to come out of nowhere.

"It's not me making the exceptions, but I can't talk about it."

"Do you want her to be your girlfriend?" I asked.

He shook his head. "No. Not even close."

"Well, how's our little heroine?" a deep voice boomed.

I looked past Sean to see Mr. T standing there, grinning broadly.

"I'm not really a heroine," I said. "I was just doing my job."

"Remember what you just said, because that'll make a good sound bite when you're interviewed."

"I'm going to be interviewed?"

"TV stations are on their way."

"Whitney spotted him. If she hadn't —"

"Whitney wants to stay low-key, so we're just going to talk about what you did. This is Amber." A young woman with short black hair and glasses stepped forward. "She's our publicist. She's going to prep you and help you through this."

"Can I stay low-key, too?" I asked.

Amber smiled. "It won't be bad. Just a few questions and a few answers."

"You can do this," Sean said.

"How do you know?"

He grinned. "I just know."

* * *

"I was just doing my job."

I didn't sound too stupid. Mom had TiVoed the news so we could watch my interview — over and over if we wanted. Although I thought once would be enough for me. We were sitting on the couch together. She was squeezing my hand, like she thought maybe the interview was going to have a bad outcome.

The camera cut away to Mr. T, looking very important as he explained how all the students who worked at the park were trained to save lives.

Mom clicked the remote and muted the TV. "I'm so proud of you," she said.

"I didn't do it alone, though," I said. "I can't figure out why Whitney didn't want any attention. And Nick called for help. He should have been on the news, too."

"They helped, but you were the one who saved the little boy's life, when you get right down to it."

"I guess."

Doing the interview hadn't been as hard as I'd expected, mostly because Sean had hung around off camera, giving me a thumbs-up, making me feel like I could do the interview — could do anything, actually.

I knew he was probably being so supportive because he was my supervisor. He'd stayed with me for the interview, then checked up on me several times throughout the afternoon. They'd had a counselor come talk to me, to help me adjust to my new heroine status and to offer guidance and an ear if I wanted to talk about what had happened, what I'd done.

He'd been helpful, but Sean sitting down with me during my break and just letting me talk it out had helped a lot more. It's kind of overwhelming to realize that you've saved a life. But talking with Sean made me realize that nothing monumental was going to change in my life.

Yes, I'd have some attention for a few days, but I was still me. And I still had a job to do.

The doorbell rang.

"I'll get it," I said. I got up off the couch, walked to the front door, and opened it.

Sean was standing there.

"Hi," I said, totally surprised to see him. As long as I'd known him he'd never actually come to my house. Stopped by to pick me up, but it was usually a quick stop at the curb and me hopping into his car so he could take Caitlin and me wherever.

"Just wanted to check, make sure you were doing all right," he said.

I smiled. "You don't have to keep checking up on me."

"I like checking up on you." He seemed embarrassed by that admission, stuck his hands in the back pockets of his jeans. "So are you gonna ride with us to work tomorrow?"

"Yeah, I thought I would. If that's okay."

"Course it's okay. I can't believe you'd think it wouldn't be."

"It's just that things have been kinda weird lately — with everyone. I can't explain it."

"I know what you mean."

Did he? Did he really? Did he know that most of that weirdness had to do with how I was feeling about him? How confused I was? Was Whitney right? Did he really like me? In that I'd-like-to-kiss-her kind of way?

"Honey, who is it?" Mom called out.

"Sean!" I yelled back.

Mom walked into the foyer. "Hi, Sean."

"Hi, Ms. Johnson."

"Why don't you come on in?"

"Uh, no thanks. I was just checking on Robyn. I need to go. See you tomorrow," he said.

He turned and headed down the sidewalk.

"Sean, wait." Closing the door behind me, I hurried to catch up with him. Then wondered what it was I thought I needed to tell him so badly. He was looking at me so intently, like he thought I was going to say something really important.

"I just wanted you to know that I don't tell Caitlin *everything*. There's been a lot lately that I haven't told her, and I just needed you to know that. Caitlin is my best friend, but you're my friend, too —" I squeezed my eyes shut. That sounded so lame.

Because I wasn't really thinking of him as a friend. I was thinking of him as more than a friend — but I didn't know how to tell him that. Or maybe I was just afraid that he'd burst out laughing.

I opened my eyes. "Anyway, I just wanted you to know that I don't tell her everything."

"That's good, because I don't tell her *anything*."

"Maybe you should. She's great at listening."

"She's great at talking. You're the one who listens."

"I can't believe how much you've noticed about me."

"I've noticed a lot — for a long time."

He turned and walked away before I could say anything. He got in his car and drove off.

I stood there for several moments wondering if maybe he'd been trying to tell me something today — by always being there, by always checking up on me. By noticing all the small things about me.

I'd told him the truth. I hadn't told Caitlin about a lot of things. But I suddenly realized that I was going to have to tell her this. I needed to tell her that I liked her brother.

The question was: How?

CHAPTER FIFTEEN

Two nights later, the park was closed to guests. The employees were hanging around, waiting for it to get dark enough for the movie to be seen on the Tsunami wall.

I was walking through the park, headed to the Tsunami lounge deck where I was going to meet up with Whitney. Caitlin had plans to stay close to Tanner, to watch the movie in a double inner tube, holding hands. Sounded romantic.

I still hadn't figured out how to tell Caitlin that I liked her brother, although I was starting to wonder if maybe I needed to tell him first. Things between us were even weirder. He said hi when I got into the car in the morning and he talked to me if something came up about the job, but other than that, he was avoiding me.

But it wasn't like he was angry with me. Or that he didn't like me.

I thought maybe he was feeling the same weirdness I was, wondering if I liked him, since I was wondering if he really liked me. As I walked past the entrance that led to the main gate, I heard *"Brawk!* Thanks, mate!"

And knew that Sean was near the gate, feeding the parrot. I thought about walking down there, talking to him, but I saw Caitlin at the water's edge of Tsunami, talking to Tanner —

Not really talking, actually. It looked like maybe she was yelling. Another girl was standing there and Tanner had his arm around her.

What was up with that?

I turned and started walking toward the wave pool. About the same time, Caitlin spun on her heels and started walking away from the pool.

"Caitlin?"

It looked like maybe she was trying not to cry. She stumbled to a stop in front of me. "Did you see him?" she asked. "Did you see him kissing her?"

I shook my head, totally confused. "No. What? Who? Tanner?"

"That skank. She works in the gift shop. He was kissing her. He's such a jerk. I want to go home."

She stormed past me, heading toward the locker room. I hurried to catch up.

"You can't go home," I said.

"Why not?" She didn't slow down.

"The movie —"

"Do you really think I care?"

She pushed on the door and disappeared inside the locker room. I glanced around and followed.

I found her sitting on a bench, her face buried in her hands.

"Caitlin?" I said softly, sitting beside her.

She lifted her tear-streaked face. "I really liked him, Robyn. He never kissed me. Why did he kiss *her*?"

"Because he's a jerk or stupid or . . . I don't know. I don't have the code to understanding guys yet."

"I don't think there is a code. But you're right. He is a jerk, just like my brother."

"No," I said sternly, so sternly that her eyes widened in surprise. "Sean isn't a jerk."

"Yes —"

"I know he's your brother, and I know he gets on your nerves but he's not a jerk. He's the reason you're working at Tsunami."

"What are you talking about?"

"He knew you wanted to work there, so he talked to the right people and made it happen."

"He never said anything —"

"Of course he didn't. He's a guy. Guys don't always talk about the good things they do. But Sean did it for you. He's nice,

Caitlin, and he cares about people and he's always there when someone needs him. He makes me smile, and sometimes he makes me laugh. And I like him. I like him a lot."

She sniffed and wiped at her tears. "What do you mean? You like him the way that I liked Tanner?"

"No, I like him differently because I know him. I don't know if you really knew Tanner."

"But I thought I did. I mean I thought I really liked him, Robyn. Why did he kiss that other girl? He and I had so much fun the other night."

I leaned over and hugged her. "I know you liked him. And I'm sorry."

She pulled back. "But you and Sean — is that why you were hanging out together at the party?"

"I don't really know anymore. I mean I thought maybe he liked me, but now's he's avoiding me. I just need you to stop calling him a jerk. Because he's not."

"This is weird. How can you like my brother?"

"I just do."

It took a while but I finally convinced Caitlin that if she left without watching the movie that Tanner would have won. I'm not sure *what* he'd have won — but it was just important that she stay.

Besides, it was a big night for Whitney and me. And even though Caitlin didn't like her as much as she liked me, our little clique of two had grown to three, even if she hadn't been around much to see it. Whitney was our friend now, and friends were there for one another.

I knew Whitney would never admit it to anyone, but she was nervous about tonight, about how our idea of a float-in movie would work.

When Caitlin and I finally met up with Whitney at the lounge chairs, Caitlin told her about what had happened with Tanner. It surprised me that she did, but

I figured she was still upset and needed to vent.

"He's obviously a dumb jock," Whitney said when Caitlin finished telling her everything. "Anyone can see that you're way better than the gift shop girl."

Caitlin seemed to perk up at that announcement. I don't know why, but Whitney had a way of saying things so there was no room for argument. If she said it, it was true.

"You're right," Caitlin said. "I'm never ever going to get involved with a jock again. As a matter of fact, I may swear off guys completely for the summer. Just wait until school starts —"

"You're overreacting," I told her.

"I'm not so sure. That article I read about summer romances was right. There's just something about the summer that turns people into idiots when it comes to love. I mean, look at you. And my brother."

"I guess." Although I didn't feel like an

idiot. And I wasn't sure what I was feeling was just a summer thing. I think maybe part of what I was feeling had been there all along.

"I can't believe you decided to stay in Mini Falls," Caitlin said. "You could have chosen anything."

"I like it there."

One of the advantages to being a park hero — other than the fact that you just feel really good for having made a difference in someone's life — was that you got to choose the area of the water park that you wanted to work in. I could have gone anywhere.

As crazy as it sounds, I told them that I wanted to stay at Splash. But since I was suddenly in a position of power, I did pull a few strings about something else.

"I'm going to go check on the movie, see how much longer before they start it," Whitney said.

"Bring us back some ice cream, will you?" Caitlin asked.

"Sure."

Whitney was eating a lot of ice cream lately. I thought maybe it had something to do with Jake.

I'd had my fifteen seconds of fame — or fifteen seconds on TV. It wasn't so bad. I didn't know why Whitney didn't want anyone to know that she'd helped, why she didn't want to be interviewed.

"So what do you think her real story is?" Caitlin asked. "Because I get the impression she's not telling us everything."

"I don't know."

"There's something going on with her," she emphasized. "That was just weird that she didn't want anyone to know she'd helped."

"We'll figure it out before the summer is over," I said with confidence.

"Yeah," she said. "We will."

A few minutes later, the Tsunami waves calmed.

Whitney came back. "It's time."

She grabbed an inner tube. "Come on."

Caitlin and I grabbed our inner tubes. She put her hand on my arm. "Just so you know, when it comes to Sean, we still have a lot to talk about. I'm talking intervention stuff here, because you're my best friend, and you can't get together with my brother."

I gave her a smile, turned, and rushed into the pool, with Caitlin following. It was strange to have her following me when I usually followed her. And I wasn't too worried about the intervention stuff. Caitlin wasn't going to change my mind about him. I knew that much for sure.

Caitlin, Whitney, and I went out pretty far, along with most of the other employees. Then we each got into our individual tubes. The night had grown dark, only a few distant lights were on. An image came up on the wall and *Jaws* began.

I heard someone scream and someone else laugh.

I didn't think anyone was going to take this movie seriously. But it was kinda cool to be watching the movie while floating in the pool.

I felt a tug on my inner tube, looked back. Sean put his finger to his lips and started pulling me back. Whitney and Caitlin were already too absorbed in the movie to notice.

When we were a good distance away, where Sean could stand in the pool while I bobbed beside him, he said, "I heard you decided to stay at Splash."

"Yeah. I like it there."

"That doesn't really work for me."

"Why not?"

He released a short burst of laughter. "You really don't know, do you?"

I thought maybe I did but I was afraid to say it in case it wasn't what I thought.

"I like you," he said.

I slid off the inner tube so I was standing in the pool in front of him. The water was lapping at my waist.

"You do?"

"I have for a long time."

"Why didn't you say something?"

"Because you're Caitlin's friend and it just seemed kinda weird, you know?"

Yeah, I did. I took a deep breath —

"I really like you, too," I confessed.

He grinned. "Enough to date me if we can figure this Caitlin thing out?"

"I don't think Caitlin is going to be a problem."

"You're going to have to leave Mini Falls, before we can do anything official."

I smiled brightly. "Actually, you're the one who's going to be leaving."

He stopped grinning. "What? What are you talking about?"

"Well, see, they were being really nice, telling me I could have anything I wanted, and Whitney told me that when you ask for stuff you're supposed to ask for the biggest thing you can think of — so I thought 'Okay, I'll do it.'"

"Do what?" he asked.

"Ask them to transfer you to marketing."

"You're kidding?" He looked surprised, his eyes big and round. I decided I liked the look.

I shook my head. "Nope. They're going to tell you tomorrow, but I wanted to tell you tonight."

"But you hate working at Splash."

"It's not so bad, and you're right. I need to work my way up. And watching the kids is an important job."

There were screams in the background as the shark attacked.

"Robyn, I can't believe you did that."

"I was being selfish, really. I didn't want you to be my supervisor — just in case, you know, we worked out our communication problem."

"You're never selfish. That's one of the reasons I like you so much. And if I'm not your supervisor anymore, well, then I can do this without getting in trouble."

He dipped his head and touched his lips to mine. My very first kiss. It was everything I thought it would be: warm and thrilling and perfect.

It felt so right, being with Sean, kissing Sean. It was difficult to imagine that I'd ever had any doubts — that I'd ever not known that he liked me, that I'd ever thought that I didn't like him.

He drew back and grinned. "I've wanted to do that for a long time."

"Is that the reason you always left the room when I walked in?"

"Yeah, I was afraid you'd figure it out — that maybe I was looking at you with longing or something like they do in the movies." He shook his head. "How embarrassing."

"If I had figured it out maybe this would have happened sooner."

"Maybe. What matters is that it's happening now."

We stood there with the water lapping around us. Screams that weren't coming from the movie and laughter echoed around us. People were having a good time. I should celebrate that the idea was a success. But all

I wanted to celebrate was Sean and me. Finally. At last.

He must have been thinking the same thing, because he leaned in and kissed me again.

I could tell already that there were going to be advantages to dating someone who'd known me forever. He knew everything about me, especially how much I liked his kisses.

TAKE A SNEAK PEEK AT

A couple of hours later, I was stretched out on a lounge chair on the Tsunami deck, eyes closed, soaking up the sun, waiting for Robyn and Whitney to catch up with me for lunch. Since this was my work area, I was always the first one to arrive. I suppose it would have been fairer to switch around where we ate, but the truth was that my area had the best views of guys.

Originally, I'd been thrilled about that aspect, but after my experience with Tanner, I was no longer sure that I wanted a summer romance. As a matter of fact, I was pretty sure I didn't. I just wanted to work, shop, hang out with friends. Maybe later, I'd take a more serious interest in guys again, maybe when school started —

"Hey, if it isn't the rules girl stretched out on my lounge chair."

I heard another lounge chair scrape over the ground as someone sat on it. Droplets of water slapped my bare arm. I'd taken off my sunglasses because I didn't want big white ovals of non-tanned skin around my eyes so I had to squint to see who had disturbed me. Although I thought I'd recognized the voice. It just sounded a little different close up, when it wasn't being yelled across water.

Romeo.

His wet hair fell across his brow again, and he did a little flick of his head to get it out of the way. More droplets slapped my arm. It appeared that keeping his hair out of his eyes was a constant battle, because almost immediately the heavy locks fell back over his forehead. His sunglasses prevented me from telling the exact color of his eyes.

When he was in the pool and not wearing shades, I could tell that they were a light color. Blue maybe. Like the sky at noon. Not that I really cared about his rebellious hair or the color of his eyes. I just wanted him to go away.

"I don't think it's yours. No towel, no bag, no item showing that you claimed this spot," I told him with authority. After all, I still had my whistle, which meant I was the girl in charge.

"Right there. My Birks."

I leaned over and looked beneath the chair, where he was pointing. No way those were there when I sat down.

I grabbed my sunglasses from where they rested beside my hip and put them on. It's easier to be intimidating when you're not squinting. "Sorry, but it doesn't count when you slip them under there *after* someone has sat down."

"Why would I do that?"

"To irritate me, because I wouldn't let you swim with Juliet on your shoulders."

"Juliet?" Then, as though a lightbulb had gone off, he grinned broadly. "That's good. Clever, even. So you caught that my name is Romeo, huh?"

"Hard to miss when your girlfriend is screaming it at the top of her lungs."

"She's not my girlfriend."

Okay, this was too much like my experience with Tanner earlier in the summer. No-commitment-Tanner as I'd started to think of him. Too-many-girls-too-little-time-Tanner. I thought of a new name for him almost every day. I knew I needed to get over what had happened, but what can I say? I was crushed.

"Does she know that?" I asked.

"I hope so. She seemed pretty smart."

I just bet. "Could you go away, because I'm trying to take a break here?"

"So what's your name?" he asked, as though I hadn't spoken, as though I wasn't trying to get him to run off and play with some other girl.

"Good-bye."

"Bummer! You've got cruel parents. What were they thinking to name you that?"

I had to fight really hard not to smile at his teasing. And talk about cruel parents. *Romeo?* But I wasn't mean enough to point that out. No reason to make him feel badly about his name just because I wanted him to leave.

Why was he even over here? I wasn't going to tease back. I wasn't going to indicate that I had any interest at all. I had a new rule: only one heartbreak per summer. I'd reached my limit.

"I bet it gets really hard when you're at a party and everyone starts leaving," he said, as though he wasn't at all bothered by my ignoring him. "I mean, you have to wonder — are they really saying good-bye or do they want to talk to *you*."

Groaning, I shook my head and closed my eyes. I wasn't going to be influenced by his cuteness or the fact that he seemed as though he might be a lot of fun. Been there, done that.

I felt a disturbance near my hip-pack — where I'd clipped my park ID earlier. My eyes sprung open in time to see him holding my ID and reading my name.

"Caitlin. I like it," he said.

"Like I care what you like," I said, shooing his hand — as though it was a pesky mosquito — away from my badge.

"So why are you giving me such a hard time?" he asked.

"You're a player. Obviously."

"Why? Because people call me Romeo?"

"You're here with another girl. Shouldn't you give attention to her?"

"Actually, I'm *not* here with another girl. I just met her this morning. We were hanging out in the pool for a while. She's off doing something else now."

Why was he telling me all this? Didn't my attitude say "I don't care"? And where were Robyn and Whitney? I sat up, looked around, and spotted them at a nearby table. Robyn wiggled her fingers at me. Great. We were supposed to be lifeguards, rescuing people. Why couldn't she and Whitney see that *I* needed rescuing?

"Gotta go," I said. "My lunch partners are here."

I picked up my soft-sided cooler.

"Later," he said.

I didn't want to be totally rude so I gave him a halfhearted wave. I crossed over the sand that made this part of the park look like an island. I dropped into the chair at the table. "Thanks, y'all, for coming to my rescue."

"I didn't realize you wanted rescuing," Robyn said.

"Well, I did."

"Who's the cutie?" Whitney asked.

"Romeo," I stated flatly.

Robyn laughed. "No way!"

"Yeah. That's what I thought. I've already had one Romeo this summer, thanks so very much."

To Do List: Read all the Point books!

By Aimee Friedman

- ☐ South Beach
- ☐ French Kiss
- ☐ Hollywood Hills
- ☐ The Year My Sister Got Lucky

☐ **Airhead**
By Meg Cabot

☐ **Suite Scarlett**
By Maureen Johnson

☐ **Love in the Corner Pocket**
By Marlene Perez

☐ **Hotlanta**
By Denene Millner and Mitzi Miller

Summer Boys series by Hailey Abbott

- ☐ Summer Boys
- ☐ Next Summer
- ☐ After Summer
- ☐ Last Summer

In or Out series by Claudia Gabel

- ☐ In or Out
- ☐ Loves Me, Loves Me Not
- ☐ Sweet and Vicious
- ☐ Friends Close, Enemies Closer

☐ **Orange Is the New Pink**
By Nina Malkin

Making a Splash series by Jade Parker

- ☐ Robyn
- ☐ Caitlin
- ☐ Whitney

Once Upon a Prom series by Jeanine Le Ny

- ☐ Dream
- ☐ Dress
- ☐ Date

SCHOLASTIC and associated logos are trademarks and/or registered trademarks of Scholastic Inc.

I ♥ Bikinis series

- ❏ **He's with Me**
  By Tamara Summers
- ❏ **Island Summer**
  By Jeanine Le Ny
- ❏ **What's Hot**
  By Caitlyn Davis

- ❏ **To Catch a Pirate**
  By Jade Parker

- ❏ **Kissing Snowflakes**
  By Abby Sher

- ❏ **The Heartbreakers**
  By Pamela Wells

- ❏ **Secret Santa**
  By Sabrina James

By Erin Haft

- ❏ **Pool Boys**
- ❏ **Meet Me at the Boardwalk**

Little Secrets series by Emily Blake

- ❏ **1: Playing with Fire**
- ❏ **2: No Accident**
- ❏ **3: Over the Edge**
- ❏ **4: Life or Death**
- ❏ **5: Nothing but the Truth**

Story Collections

- ❏ **Fireworks: Four Summer Stories**
  By Niki Burnham, Erin Haft, Sarah Mlynowski, and Lauren Myracle
- ❏ **21 Proms**
  Edited by Daniel Ehrenhaft and David Levithan
- ❏ **Mistletoe: Four Holiday Stories**
  By Hailey Abbott, Melissa de la Cruz, Aimee Friedman, and Nina Malkin

Point

www.thisispoint.com